Lila, the Revolutionary

A Fable

William T.
Hathaway

www.peacewriter.org

Lila, the Revolutionary

A Fable

William T.
Hathaway
www.peacewriter.org

Nascent Books
www.nascentbooks.com

Nascent Books

St Albert, AB, Canada

www.nascentbooks.com

Nascent Books is an imprint of Avatar Publications, Canada

First Nascent Books Print Edition 2014

Cover photo by Ferdinand Reus licensed under Creative Commons.

Cover design by Michael Sosteric (mikes.sociology.org)

Cover font Chavez Pro by Trinchera (http://www.trincheracreativa.com/)

Chapter opener image by Glentamara licensed under public domain via Wikimedia Commons.

978-1-897455-83-8   Lila (PDF)
978-1-897455-84-5   Lila (Print)

Dedication

For Daniela Rommel and
Bob Schuster

Acknowledgment

The author would like to thank Jim and Herdis
Burkard for their friendship and help with the
manuscript.

Preface

"The world can only be changed by people who don't like it," wrote Bertolt Brecht in explaining why radicals have a negative attitude about the society we live in. We don't like the way things are. Sometimes our dislike can even become loathing.

It was in just such a fit of loathing that the idea for *Lila, the Revolutionary* came to me. I was appalled by how capitalism has become so pervasive and aggressive, a globalized madness. In despair, I saw all these predatory men and women in dark suits commanding us, marching us resolutely towards war and poverty. They're so powerful and blind...and they're everywhere. What's the way out of this? How can we overthrow this murderous system? Then a phrase from the Bible in the came to me: "A little child shall lead them."

The idea of a child leading a revolution was so farfetched that I knew there must be something to it. After all, we adults haven't managed it so well. But I wondered, What kind of a child could lead a revolution? A little girl popped into my mind and said, "*Me!*" What's your name? I asked her. "*Lila.*" How old are you? "*I'm eight.*" How are you going to lead the revolution? "*I'll tell you about it."* And she did.

The story is set in an unspecified neocolonial country, which gives it a universal quality. Only Lila has a personal name; the others are named after their relationship to her, as the way children see the world. Like most fables, it doesn't abide by the conventions of literal realism.

Lila, the Revolutionary embodies an esthetic different from and opposed to mainstream art and entertainment, which seek to distract us from the worsening conditions of our lives and render us incapable of changing them. These diversions lull us with subjective emotions that offer solace and escape from our objective reality. They range from the crude to the refined, but all are characterized by glorifying the inner life of the supposedly sovereign individual. This esthetic trend, part of the romantic movement, began with the ascendency of capitalism and expressed the self-oriented mentality of the rising bourgeoisie. The new rulers supported institutions and art that reflected their personalities: extreme individuality that rejected all fetters and pursued its desires regardless of the consequences for others. In exalting the superior autonomous spirit over the mediocre masses, it served to isolate the growing socialist movement. By the mid nineteenth century this had trickled down to become a widespread mentality of the educated population, cutting them off from the working class. Marx summed it up: "The ruling ideology is always the ideology of the rulers."

As the crises of capitalism deepened in the twentieth century, the emphasis on subjectivity increased, especially in the realms of art and philosophy. The inner world, the joys and pains of our private emotions, was portrayed as the highest and most authentic topic for art. The artist became the new priest, guiding us to sublime planes of existence. This prevailing esthetic allowed us to leave the crass social reality behind and become an aristocrat of the spirit. It generated passivity and turned the personal life into a refuge from and a substitute for the public life. This trend has now reached its effete endstage in postmodernism with its deconstruction of reality into conceptual narratives which have only subjective meanings.

We are saturated with art and entertainment that tell us to shun the social deterioration surrounding us and focus instead on romance, violence, and the shimmers of our interior zones, while outside the conditions of our lives are gradually being degraded. Our eyes are captivated by images on electronic screens and our minds captivated by hyper-stimulated feelings flooding our mental screen. We are losing the capacity for clear thinking and objective analysis, so effective action is slipping from our grasp.

We are in desperate need of an esthetic that will enable us to recognize our calamitous situation, identify the causes of it, and act to change it. Once we can understand how destructive capitalism really is, the necessity of democratic socialism will be obvious.

Some works of art do criticize the system, protest it, and urge reforms, but very few challenge it fundamentally. Instead they seek to improve it. But this gradual ameliorative approach has been tried for over a century now and has yielded only superficial changes. Capitalism can't be fixed from the inside; it is inherently savage and must be replaced.

The qualities of a radical esthetic are described by David Walsh, arts editor of the World Socialist Web Site: "True art in the modern world necessarily must be revolutionary. It is impossible to produce a significant work of art without taking a rejection of the injustice and irrationality of modern life as a starting point. Further, this rejection must be informed by a revolutionary political perspective if it is not to lapse into hopelessly idealistic clichés."

Jack London's *The Iron Heel* and B. Traven's jungle novels are steps in this direction. They show the necessity of moving beyond criticism, protest, and reform towards building a mass movement that can eventually overthrow the government and the corporations it serves. *Lila* tries to take this impulse another step forward, and I hope you can take it farther.

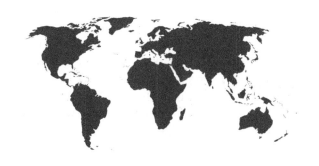

In a land both far away and near.
In a time both future and now.
In a struggle that is all of us.

Lila reached up and scratched the cow's forehead the way she liked it, then stroked her cinnamon fur smooth. Their four brown eyes met in wordless communication. Lila was smiling and she thought the cow was smiling too. Cows smile differently from people; you can't see it so much as feel it. The way the cow gazed at her and swung her tail told Lila she was happy. When Lila poured a bucket of oats into the manger of her stall, she got even happier. Her nostrils widened and she snorted and stamped the ground with her hoof. Her long pink tongue licked at the oats, and her beige lips plunged into them. She hummed deep in her throat.

While the cow was eating, Lila set the

empty bucket under the water pump. She pressed with both hands as hard as she could on the pump handle. The pipe coughed and gurgled, then splashed water into the bucket, smelling of iron and earth. She poured this and three more loads into the water trough, put the bucket away, and picked up the scoop next to the bag of chicken feed. She thrust the scoop deep into the seeds and grains but then poured some back as she remembered her mother saying, "Don't give them too much." With the scoop half full she walked out of the cow shed and over to the chicken coop, whistling to them through her chipped tooth. The birds ran clucking towards her, some flapping their wings in eagerness. "Breakfast, birdies!" she called and flung the food in a wide arc over them, scattering it far enough so they wouldn't fight over it. The ducks who'd been floating on the tilapia pond took off and flew the ten meters, landed on the run, and began gobbling and quacking.

Lila squatted, wrapped her arms around her knees, and leaned back on her heels to be on their level to watch them eat. The birds trotted around, eyes glued to the ground, eating as fast and as much as they could. A half scoop wasn't really enough for six chickens and two ducks, but her mother said they couldn't afford more and the chickens should work harder to find bugs. The ducks, according to mother, were unwelcome guests. They had just shown up one day at the pond and were eating the fish the family needed. Although their eggs were larger than chicken eggs, they hid them so they were harder to find. Mother told her she should scare them away, but Lila couldn't do that. She wished she could cluck in duck language and tell them to leave before they ended up in the soup pot. They always had a silly but friendly smile on their faces, but that was probably just the way their bills were shaped. Unlike the cow, they didn't act particularly happy. They were all business, waddling around and gobbling everything they could. She liked their shiny green and blue feathers and had several in her collection. The chickens looked a bit mean down here at their level. Their beaks were sharp, and they kept nervously darting their heads and stepping in quick jerks as they searched for food. But she knew they weren't mean. They were chickens and chickens just look that way. She had lots of their feathers in her collection, but they weren't as special as the ducks'. Their babies were as dear as anything she'd ever seen—dear as kittens. But she didn't like to think of the two together.

Lila had asked her father once if they could have a cat, but he said the only way they could afford a cat was if they had mice in the house. No mice—no cat. Same with a dog. No robbers—no dog.

11

Two crows dived out of the sky and began strutting around plucking seeds and cawing to scare away the other birds. Lila ran at them, crying, "Get away, you!" They flapped off on their black wings and settled in the corn field with a few nasty caws. A feather from one of them floated down. Lila picked it up, black glinting blue in the sun, and stuck it in her wavy dark hair. *I'll be the crow girl—but I won't bully the other birdies.*

The seven hectares of land the family owned were planted in corn. Now it wasn't even as tall as she was, but in the fall when it was taller even than her parents, men would come with a big machine and cut it all down and give them money. The whole family worked to take care of the corn: pulling weeds, pumping water, putting on special chemicals this kind of corn needed. Lila didn't have to work too much on the corn because she was only eight and still going to school. But her brother was sixteen and had just stopped school so he could work more and help the family. Her grandfather owned the farm, but he was old now, so her mother and father did most of the work.

Lila remembered when she was little they grew lots of vegetables and fruit—sold some, ate the rest. But that didn't bring enough money, so now it was all corn that got sent away to another country for animal feed, and they bought food from the store. They had milk from the cow, though, and fish from the pond, eggs from the chickens, and when a chicken got too old to lay eggs, they had chicken soup. Soon maybe duck soup, but Lila didn't want to think about that. Maybe if she worked extra hard to find all their eggs, her mother would let the ducks stay.

She walked over to the blossoming fig tree and sat in the swing that hung from the largest limb. She loved to swing and was now big and strong enough to do it by herself. She pulled on the rope with her arms and pushed with her legs, going back and forth higher and higher until it seemed she could fly into the air, over the house and fields, fly like the ducks and crows, much higher than the clumsy chickens. Once she had tried that, jumping off the swing at the highest point, but instead of flying she had fallen and chipped her front tooth. The tooth had already fallen out and grown back once, and she thought it would do that again. She cried when mother told her no, that only happens once. Since then she flew only with her mind, not her body.

"Lila, come in," father called from the porch of their house. "We need to get ready to go." Today was a festival, and they were going to ride the bus into the city for music and games in the park.

She dragged her heels on the ground to slow down, then jumped off and ran to the house.

Its plaster, once white, was now gray and had crumbled off in places, uncovering the stones beneath. Instead of climbing the steps, she reached her hands up towards her father, who grabbed them and swung her onto the wooden porch, both of them laughing.

Inside, mother was packing a basket of food for the day. "I ironed your special blouse," mother told her. "It's in your room." Lila went into the small room she shared with her brother, who was sitting on her bed, the lower bunk, brushing his shoes to shine them. She took the blouse, which mother had embroidered for her eighth birthday, into the bathroom and put it on. It was pretty but too big. Mother said that was so she could grow into it.

As she came out, father told her, "Go make sure grandpa's ready. We have to leave or we'll miss the bus."

Lila knocked on the door of grandpa's room at the front of the house. He didn't answer, so she went in, asking, "Ready to go?" First she noticed a chair lying on the floor, then she saw grandfather swinging slowly back and forth, feet not touching the floor, a rope tied from his neck to a ceiling beam. Lila screamed and ran to him, tried to lift him up from the rope, but she wasn't strong enough. She cried out again and fell to the floor as her parents rushed in. They both gasped then wailed as they saw the body, now swinging wider

14

from Lila's attempt to free it. Eyes filled with tears, they held grandpa up away from the rope, but his head sagged limply to the side. "Father!" Lila's father cried, "Not this! No!"

Her brother stood in the door, eyes wide, mouth gaping. Mother called to him, "Bring a knife, quick!"

Lila's father was holding on to his father and crying, head against his chest. Mother was holding on to her husband and crying, head against his shoulder. Lila knelt on the floor crying and holding on to her parents' legs. Grandpa hung above, looking down on them with bulging eyes.

Brother ran in with a knife, and father stood on the chair and cut the rope. Mother and brother held the body and eased it down onto the floor. Lila picked up her grandpa's hand, then dropped it because it was cold and lifeless. The cold seemed to creep inside her and freeze something.

Father took a sheet of paper off the desk.

"Did he leave a note?" mother asked.

"No," father said, "just this." He showed them a printed letter and read, "Notice of foreclosure of mortgage."

Mother closed her eyes and her head sank.

"What does that mean?" Lila asked.

"It means we don't own this farm and house anymore. We have to leave," father said in a stunned whisper, face creased.

"Did somebody take it?" Lila asked.

"The bank took it." Father's word's came slowly. "Grandpa had to borrow money from the bank to buy the special corn seeds. Then he had to borrow more money to buy the chemicals the seeds need to grow and to kill the bugs. Before they loaned him the money, the bank made him sign that they could take the farm and house if he didn't pay it back. He thought he would be able to pay it back because the seed company said their seeds would produce lots of corn. But they didn't." Father shook his head back and forth and squeezed his hands together. "They actually produced less than the old kind of seeds. So he didn't get enough money to pay the bank back. He was trying to get them to wait so he could pay them later. We talked about it...how worried he was, but he hoped they would wait. But now we know they didn't. Now they own all this...and they want us to go."

"Can we fight them?" brother asked.

"No," father answered. "I wish we could. But they have the police and soldiers on their side." He put one arm around his son and his hand on his daughter's head as she sat on the floor. "We didn't want you to worry about this, so we didn't tell you."

Lila stared up at him. "Where will we go?"

"We will have to move into the city, try to find work there."

Mother cried louder. "We are not city people. The city is brutal." She sank to her knees beside grandpa. "Why did you do this? You should have stayed with us. We would do better together."

"He was too ashamed," father said. "But you're right, he shouldn't have done it. I didn't think he would. But I didn't think the bank would actually take our farm either. I thought they'd give us a chance."

"What will they do with it?" brother asked.

"Whatever will bring them the most money," father said. He reached down and lifted Lila up onto her feet. "I'm sorry you had to find him...a terrible shock to you. Go out and play now."

"I can't play," she said. As father led her out, she looked at grandpa sprawled on the floor. He would never get up from there. That's what it meant to be dead. She wouldn't see him again...ever. Where did he go? Did he just fly away? Her tears streamed more and she threw herself onto the couch with a wail. Father picked up the telephone and pushed numbers. He said something into the phone, but she was crying too loud to hear. Everything she saw reminded her of grandfather: his favorite chair in the corner, his place at the head of the dinner table, his smiling face in family photos on the wall, his coat hanging by the front door. She ran out the back door, but in the yard she saw the fig tree with her swing, and she remembered him making it for her then pushing her in it, both of them laughing. The rope on the tree reminded her of the rope from the ceiling, and she cried louder. She couldn't stand it. How could a person not be there anymore?

Something seemed to be closing around her, crushing her, squeezing everything together into a hard little ball. She didn't want to be that hard little ball. She dropped to the ground and beat with her hands and kicked with her legs. The feather fell out of her hair. Even the hard little ball was being crushed into dust that would blow away. She'd be gone like grandpa. Lila brought her knees up to her chest, clenched her arms around her legs, held herself tightly to keep from disappearing, and said her name over and over: "Lila...Lila...."

They buried grandfather beneath the fig tree. Father had built the coffin and mother had lined it with green cloth, grandpa's favorite color. Brother had dug the deep hole. Lila had mostly cried. 150 people came to wish him farewell.

Many of them told stories about things he'd done and said, and how much they liked and missed him. Four women were there whose husbands had also killed themselves because they couldn't pay their debts. The bank had taken their land, and some of them now lived with their children under a bridge by the river. One man told how he had sold a part of his body — a kidney — to pay his debt. Rich people whose kidneys were broken buy them. But now he wasn't strong enough to work his land, so he was trying to sell the farm and move his family into the city.

"What is it like in the city?" Lila asked.

The people were quiet. Then one said, "You have to work very hard to get enough to eat." Another said, "You have to live many people in one room." "And it is always noisy," someone added. "And hard to breathe...so many cars," said a fourth.

Lila's brother kicked the ground with his sandal. "We won't move. We'll just stay here. We'll tell the bank no."

The people shook their heads, and father said, "Then they will come with police and push us out."

Lila thought father looked old now, almost as old as grandpa.

"That is what they do," a woman said. "And they can give you a fine so you have even less money."

Brother didn't say anything, just pushed his teeth into his lower lip.

"What about the cow and chickens?" Lila asked. "Can we take them with us?"

"No," father said, "we have to sell them to

pay for the move."

Lila had never seen such a tall building. She counted eight stories, one for each year she'd been alive. They lived in the middle. She and her brother had a room just big enough for their double-deck bunks and a little table. The living room was bigger, so mother and father slept there on the couch that folded out into a bed. They had to move the TV every night to make room.

Lila could lean out the window into the gray air and see little people below on the sidewalk scurrying around like mice, always in a hurry. The different colored tops of the cars moved and stopped like pieces in a video game. Pigeons and sparrows flew back and forth between the roof of the building and the garbage on the street. She did find a nice pigeon feather, though, which she put in the old candy box that held her collection. The apartment was like a cage to her. She couldn't just run out the door and play. Six blocks away was a small park with swings, but it was always crowded, you had to wait for a swing, and the other kids would yell at you if they thought you were swinging too long. They weren't very nice. There was a seesaw, but it was broken. She wanted to learn to swim, and there was a pool in town, but it cost money.

Her mother got a job right away because she was good at sewing. She had made clothes for the family with her own sewing machine, the kind you pedal. Now she was sewing on a big electric machine in a huge room with a hundred other women, making shirts and pants. It was noisy and hot and she had to work very fast and be careful not to sew her finger.

This didn't pay enough for the family to live on, so they were worried. At first father couldn't find work because all he knew was farming. But then he got a job in a shoe factory operating a machine that stuck the soles onto the shoes. The machine was very hot and would burn you if you didn't watch out. It gave off fumes from the hot rubber and plastic, so he coughed a lot now. But they had enough to live on, so they weren't as worried. Then father got brother a job sweeping the floors in the factory. Now they had enough money so they could save a little.

Lila still had to go to school. In the country she had liked school and wanted to go to college. Her parents said college was very expensive, and they couldn't afford it, but if she earned some money now, they could save that so she could learn to be a secretary. The factory where father and brother worked had a school where children also worked half the day. It was supposed to be practical training in business for them, and they got paid a little money, plus the parents didn't have to pay for a baby-sitter because the children were in the factory all day. In the mornings they worked in a big room with eighty children putting laces on shoes and packing them in boxes. If they did it wrong, they didn't get money. Then in the afternoons they sat in the same room for lessons. The children were different ages, so sometimes Lila knew that lesson already and other times she didn't know what the teacher was talking about. Some of the children were too tired from working and put their heads on the table and slept.

Lila's life had turned terrible. She had been happy and now she was unhappy. Before, she hadn't known she was happy. She just was it. But now that she was unhappy, she knew what she had lost.

The whole family was unhappy. They were always tired, and they got mad about little things and yelled at one another. Brother was mean to her. If she did something he didn't like, he would push her or hit her. He said he was making five times more money than she was, and that meant he should have his way. Father's mouth was usually turned down, one side lower than the other, and his eyes seemed narrower. Mother's face looked pinched, with lines showing on her forehead, tendons standing out on her neck, skin around her eyes wrinkled.

Her parents argued a lot now. Yesterday it was about rice. Mother had bought a small bag of rice, and father got angry because those were more expensive. She said the big bags were too heavy for her to carry home after work. Maybe he should buy the rice. He got mad and said the store was in the other direction from where he worked and that would make him even later getting home. He finally agreed to do it, but he was still mad. When her parents fought, Lila wanted to shrivel away and disappear.

Tonight at dinner father got mad because the plate mother gave him wasn't totally clean. She apologized but said she had to wash the dishes in a hurry and couldn't always inspect each one. He said she was a poor housekeeper. She said he never cared about her problems, just his own. He said he wished he'd never seen her in his life. She cried and threw the plate on the floor. He jumped up shaking his fist and trembling. They said terrible things to each other until father ran out the door, face red. Tears streaming, mother cleared away the mess and went into the kitchen. Brother turned on the TV loud and sat on the couch. Lila ran into the bedroom and threw herself down on her bunk. Pounding her fists on the bed, she bit into the pillow and screamed.

Her life kept getting worse and worse, and she couldn't do anything to make it better. Helpless. What was next? Maybe her parents would get divorced. Maybe they would kill themselves. She would go to an orphanage and have to work lacing and packing shoes all day. Then she would kill herself. Maybe grandpa was right — the only solution. But she didn't want to die — she hadn't even been alive for very long. Lila cried and cried until she couldn't anymore. She doubled up into a ball, squeezing herself to keep from disappearing and to drive away the thoughts.

Lila made a friend, a girl who lived on the same floor. She was ten, which was a lot older than Lila, but they could play together. They chalked hopscotch squares on the floor of the hall and had fun jumping and picking up things while standing on one foot. Usually the friend won, but she didn't laugh at Lila.

The hall didn't smell very good, though, because the door on the garbage chute was broken. After a week the building manager made them stop because the chalk messed up the floor. They could still play jacks and jump rope, though, and slide down the banisters on the stairs, if no adults were watching.

Lila, her father, and brother rode the bus to work in the mornings. At the shoe factory they and almost everyone went in through big double doors in back of the building, but Lila saw a few people going in the front door, and she asked her father why.

"Those are the managements," he told her. "They get to use that door."

"Why?" she asked.

"They don't like it where we are because it's noisy and smelly."

"I don't like it either," brother said.

"Me neither," father said with a shrug, "but we can't do anything about it."

She stared up at him. "Why not?"

As they talked, they wended their way through the crowded entry hall to the lockers, where they put their coats and lunches.

"Because they're managements," father said. "They decide how things are going to be."

"Why them?" Lila wanted to know.

"They had the money to go to college and learn how to be that."

"How did they get the money?"

"Usually they got it from their parents, and their parents got it from their parents. I'm sorry I don't have any to give you both." Father put his arms around his daughter and son and shook his head. "Some families have money, and they can use it to make more money."

"How do they do that?" Lila asked.

Father waved his hands at her. "I can't answer all your questions. We have to go to work." He picked her up and kissed her on the cheek. "But I can tell you, they didn't do it by working at jobs like we have."

After work the three of them met by the bus stop as usual. Father nervously motioned them to come with him away from the crowd at the bus stop. When they were by themselves, he said in a low voice that they weren't going straight home as usual. Instead they were going to see the man who had taken their home and land. Father had his name from the foreclosure paper and had found out which bank branch he worked at. Today was one of the days banks were open late so people could deposit their money.

Lila got scared. Anyone who would do what he had done must be a very bad man and might hurt them now.

Brother, though, was happy. "Good! I will spit in his face."

Father pushed the air with his open hands as if to brush brother's words away. "No spitting, no hitting! If we touch him or threaten him, we can go to jail and get a fine. We will just tell him what he has done to us and what we think of him. He needs to know that."

They rode a bus through heavy traffic: hulking trucks, beat-up old cars, a few new cars, tractors, three-wheeled pedicabs painted with magic charms, motor bikes and regular bikes with two or three people perched precariously. Everyone who had a horn was honking it. Finally they got off in a business district at the edge of the city. It wasn't as crowded and noisy as where they lived, the buildings weren't as high, and the air was a little better. The bank branch was in a row of stores and offices.

Inside, father asked at the front desk to speak with the man. The receptionist said he was busy and could she help him. Father said he needed to speak with him personally and it wouldn't take much time. The woman said he was the manager and surely father could understand he was very busy. Father said they would wait. The woman said the branch manager didn't speak with individual customers; father would have to either speak to someone else or leave. Father said they would stay. The woman said that was not allowed. Father said he would go find the manager himself. The woman said, no, he would not. She waved to a man standing in the corner, who walked over to them. He was a big man with a pistol and a club hanging from his belt. He told father if he didn't leave right away, he would go to jail. Everyone in the bank was looking at them now. Father's face was red and he was breathing hard through his mouth. Brother stood beside him with his fists balled. The man pointed to the door and put his other hand on his pistol. "Out!" he ordered. Father bit his lip, gestured to brother and Lila to follow, and walked with his head down towards the door. Brother spat at the man, but he was too far away and it splatted on the floor.

Outside, brother said, "I'm going to try to find his car. The manager might have a special parking space."

"No!" father said, but brother ran around to the parking lot at the side of the building. He was looking at the cars when the side door of the bank opened, and the guard ran out, grabbing at the club on his belt. Brother put up his fists to fight. Still running, the guard jabbed him in the stomach with the club. Brother screamed and fell to the ground. The guard kicked him. "Get out!"

Moaning and vomiting, brother crawled out of the parking lot. Father helped him to his feet. The guard shook his club at them. "If I ever see any of you here again, you're in jail!"

Father and Lila helped brother walk to the bus stop. "I know his car," brother said through gasps of pain. "'Manager' — right next to the door."

"Come with me," brother told Lila after work a few days later. "I borrowed a moped from a friend. We're going to follow the manager's car and find his house. Then father can go there and tell him what he has done to us."

Lila shook her head. "The man with the club...he will hit you again...and put us in jail."

"No, he won't see us," brother said. "We'll hide across the street...just watch for the car."

"I don't want to go."

"You need to go. You have to help father remove the shame these people have put on us. Otherwise you're on their side."

Lila didn't want to be on their side, but she was afraid of the man with the club.

"I'll be careful. And we have the moped to get away if anything happens," brother continued. "Come on...or we'll be late."

Lila rode on the back of the moped, holding on to her brother as he drove out to the bank along streets lined with bazaars, food stalls, and old apartment buildings. He parked across the street and down the block from the bank. Hidden between two cars, they could see the driveway of the parking lot, and they watched and waited as cars drove in and out. Lila got hungry, but brother had brought cookies, so that helped. Finally brother said, "That's it! His car!"

A plain-looking white sedan pulled out of the driveway. Brother started the moped, and they followed, leaving one car between them and the bank manager's. Traffic was thick, so they moved slowly. The car ahead of them stopped at the yellow light while the manager drove on. Brother tried to swing around the car in time to slip through, but cross traffic filled the intersection. The manager turned right and disappeared.

At the green brother sped forward to the street the manager had turned onto. Lila's dark-brown hair flew in the wind. His car was still in sight, but now with several others behind it. Darting around them, brother pulled closer but still left one car ahead. He laughed in satisfaction that they hadn't lost him. They followed him out to a neighborhood of big houses with gates and fences around them. The manager slowed in front of one of the houses. The gate to the driveway opened automatically, he drove in, the gate closed behind him, the garage door opened, he drove inside, the garage door closed.

Brother drove past the house. Lila was relieved because she'd been afraid he was going to try to go inside. He turned a corner and parked the moped on another street. "Why do we stop here?" Lila asked.

Brother locked the moped. "He might've seen us behind him. Now he'll think we just drove on."

They walked back around the corner with Lila getting nervous. The flat-roofed, two-story, white-plastered house reminded Lila of a sugar cube. A high green metal fence cut it off from the street and its neighbors.

Brother wrote down the address. "Now father can come here and tell him what he did to us. And if he won't listen to father, I will burn his house down. He took our house—I will take his house."

A police car drove past them on patrol, slowed, stopped, then backed up to where they were standing. The policeman spoke from his open window: "You children don't live here. Do you work here?"

"No," brother said.

"Then what are you doing here?" the policeman asked.

"Taking a walk," brother said.

"Well, you go take a walk in your own neighborhood," the policeman said.

"Why can't we be here?" brother asked.

"You don't belong here."

The front door of the house opened. The manager walked out towards them and asked through the fence, "Any trouble, officer?"

"No," the policeman said, "just some little beggars."

The manager was short with dark hair and a mustache. He looked like their father, except for his white shirt and tie. He smiled down at Lila. "Well, I'll give you both a little something, then you go home." He took a wallet from his pants, pulled out some bills, and handed them through the fence. Brother took them eagerly. The manager gave a friendly laugh. "Young man, you be sure to divide those equally. Just because you're bigger doesn't mean you get more." He reached through the fence and patted Lila on the head. "Now you go home and do your school work so you can get a good job and won't need to beg for money." He turned and walked contentedly back into his house.

The policeman looked at them sternly. "Don't get the idea that means you should come back here and beg again. Give me your ID cards." They handed them to him, and he held each one against the screen of a pocket computer. "I will take you home."

"We have a moped," brother said.

"Where?"

"Around the corner."

"Get in." The policeman opened the door, and brother and Lila got on the front seat. Mounted on the driver's door were a shotgun and a club; the radio was squawking and spitting static; lights flashed on the dashboard. "You're lucky he's a nice man."

They drove around the corner, and brother pointed to the moped. Brother and Lila got out and drove away on it. The policeman followed them until they were away from the big houses, then he turned back. As soon as he was gone, brother stopped and counted the money. "It's more than I make all day," he said, amazed.

Lila counted on her fingers. "It's more than I make all week. But it's only half, because we have to share it." She held out her hand, and brother reluctantly divided the bills. "Is he a nice man or a bad man?" she asked.

"I don't know. Maybe he's both," brother said, then thought a moment. "But he's more bad than nice. Our farm was worth a lot more than what he gave us now."

"Why didn't you tell him how bad he is?"

"I was afraid he'd take the money back."

"Do you still want to burn his house?"

"I want to, but now I can't," brother said. "They know who we are."

Lila heard shouting and crying coming from the hall outside their apartment. She opened the door and saw police and angry people. At first she thought they had come for her, but then she recognized her friend's family. The mother was crying, the father was shouting and shaking his fist, and a policeman was shaking his head. Her friend stood off to the side clutching her dolls and crying. Through sobs she told Lila her family had to leave. Her father had been working in a factory making umbrellas, but the company found another country where they could make them cheaper, so they fired all the workers and were moving the whole factory there. Her father had tried to get another job but couldn't. Her mother was pregnant with another baby, so no place would give her a job. Since they couldn't pay the rent, they had to move out.

Men were hauling their furniture into the freight elevator. The father started arguing with the building manager, who said he couldn't do anything about it.

Lila asked her friend where they were going to move, but she didn't know. She said she would come back and visit Lila, though, if she could.

Lila was lacing shoes. She had to make sure the laces lay flat and came out even at the ends, then pack each pair in a box. She had to do it very fast and it was very boring. A lady kept walking around to make sure everyone was lacing and packing. If you weren't, you got a warning. If you got three warnings in a day, you didn't get any pay. Another lady came around to check the shoes in the boxes. If they weren't laced right or put in the box right, you got a warning. If you got three warnings in a day, you didn't get any pay. The lady put the lids on the boxes and stacked them on a big cart she pushed around.

Lila had a headache from the way the shoes smelled and a rash on her fingers from the dyes. But mainly she was worried, afraid they would get thrown out of their apartment, afraid her mother and father would get divorced, afraid her brother would end up in jail. Maybe the whole family would end up in jail. Would she have to lace shoes the whole day there and not have any school at all? The factory was already like a jail— she couldn't leave it all day long. She and the other children got fifteen minutes in the morning, after lunch, and in the afternoon to run around outside, but everybody had to stay inside the fence. At least she got to go home at night, though. Maybe jail was like a factory where you could never go home. That would be terrible. She had thought things now were as bad as they could get, but jail sounded worse. And maybe there were things even worse than jail.

She had talked to her dolls about all this, but that didn't help. The dolls didn't seem to be alive anymore like they had been before; they seemed to be just stuffed cloth and plastic that stared at her without saying anything. She put them in her closet next to the old candy box that held her feather collection.

Lila felt she was sinking down into a pool of mud that would cover her over and she would breathe in the mud and it would fill her up until she was just mud.

The lady hit her desk with a stick and gave her a warning for not working.

Mother had run the sewing machine needle through two of her fingers and they had become infected, so now she had a fever and had to take pills and her hand was swollen and wrapped in a bandage so she couldn't work. Since she wasn't making money, they weren't sure how they could pay the rent.

All this made mother mad. Since she had

been injured at work, the company should pay her something while she was recovering. She talked to other women who had been injured — almost everybody — and they wrote a petition to management asking for accident insurance. Many women didn't want to sign it because they were afraid of being fired. More than half did sign it, though, and mother and two others gave it to the department chief, who said he would give it to the personnel chief.

A week later a notice appeared on the bulletin board saying since the injuries were caused by personal negligence, the company could not be responsible for the lost earnings. They were already generously paying for the medical expenses. They suggested the workers take out individual insurance and gave a list of agencies.

This made mother even madder. She invited six of the women who had worked on the petition to their apartment to talk about what they could do. Father and brother went out to a movie to make room for them, but Lila stayed, sitting on the green hemp couch between two of them. Most of the women had scars on their hands, and one had a finger missing. A woman with a red welt on her wrist told Lila that what she hoped most was that her daughter and Lila didn't have to do this when they grew up.

Lila said she liked to sew.

The women were silent for a moment, then one said, as if she were remembering something from long ago, she used to like to sew too. The others nodded in agreement. Then mother said it wasn't the sewing itself that was bad. It was having to do it so fast for so long in the hot noisy crowded room always under pressure from the inspectors, all this for so little money with no insurance—that's what was so awful.

"I work in the ironing section," said the woman with the welt on her wrist. "It's sweltering hot in there and we get burned on the machines, plus we have to breathe the fumes from the chemicals they use to make the cloth smooth. Almost everybody who works there has migraines. They won't even give us good fans and ventilation."

"Why does it have to be that way?" Lila asked. "Why can't you work slower in a nice room?"

The women were silent again until one with gray hair and a wrinkled face explained, "That's how the company gets its money. They pay us only a little, but they sell the things for much more...and then keep the difference. The work we do makes the things valuable, but we don't get that money, they do. Our work is their profit."

Lila hopped off the couch and paced around the khaki-colored jute rug while thoughts raced around her head and tumbled out in words: "But that's stealing from us—we made it worth more."

"They don't call it stealing, they call it profit," the woman said.

"What work do they do?"

"They don't have to work. They own the company, it all belongs to them, so they get the money. That's why they don't want to pay us more or give us insurance, because then they would have less."

The other women sat silently, glancing from the old woman to the young girl.

"Who are they?" Lila asked. "Are they the managements?"

"No, the owners don't live here. They live far away."

"Is that so they won't get put in jail for stealing from us?"

"The government says that isn't stealing," the woman said.

"It is stealing!" Lila insisted. "If our work makes the things worth more, but they take that money instead of paying it to us, that's stealing."

"Well, you're right. But we can't do anything about it," the woman said.

"Why not?"

"Because they own the company and they can do what they want."

"How did they get the company?" Lila asked.

"They bought shares in it," the woman

explained. "Each share is a little bit of the company, and they buy many shares."

"But if they buy them with money they stole from us, they don't really own it. We own it."

"Well, you're right."

"Then we have to take it back."

"They would put us in jail."

"But they're the crooks."

"Not according to the law. They make the law," the woman said.

"I thought the government makes the law."

"They own the government. They own everything."

"Even us?"

The woman nodded. "We need to do what they say to live."

"Then it really isn't our life." Lila turned to her mother. "Is that why grandpa killed himself?"

Mother nodded. "Something like that."

Lila paused, trying to figure this out. "Wouldn't it have been better if he'd tried to take it back from them? Even if he got put in jail. I'd rather visit him in jail than have him dead."

One of the younger women frowned at Lila and said, "They might put you in jail too."

"Then we'd be there together," Lila said. "But maybe we would win and take our company back from them."

"Then they could even shoot you," the young woman said.

"Then we'd be dead together. But maybe we would win."

The old woman smiled at her and said, "You understand a lot for your age."

But another one shook her finger at Lila and told her, "Young lady, you're going to get into real trouble!"

Brother had been doing a good job at work, so he was put on the night cleaning crew. It paid a little more, but he didn't get home until very late. Lila woke up each time he came into their room and climbed up into his bunk. One night he came in breathing hard and laughing to himself. She sleepily asked what had happened. Whispering so their parents wouldn't hear, he told her he'd stolen a computer.

"Turn on the light," she said. "I want to see it." He did and showed her a laptop that looked almost new. "How did you do it?" she asked.

He'd been planning it for a week, he told her. Part of his job was emptying all the waste baskets in management, dumping them into a big trash can he pushed around on a cart. For several days he kept seeing a small computer sitting beside a desk, and tonight he had put it in the trash can, hiding it under the papers. Tonight was also the night when he had to break down all the used cardboard boxes for the week and tie them in stacks for the recyclers. As he did this, he wrapped cardboard around the laptop and put it in the middle of a stack, then covered the sides of the stack with more cardboard so no one could see in. He marked the stack with a red felt pen so he could tell it from the others, loaded the stacks onto the cart, and wheeled them to the factory gate, where the guard searched him as usual to make sure he wasn't stealing. The guard never bothered with the cardboard stacks, though. Brother wheeled them down the driveway through the parking lot and unloaded them by the street, far enough away so the guard couldn't see them. The recyclers would pick them up there in the morning.

When his shift was over, he and the rest of the crew got searched as always at the gate as they were leaving.

He didn't ride the bus home. Instead he had borrowed his friend's moped again and hidden it near the factory. When everyone else had left on the bus, he had gone back to the cardboard stacks, cut open the one with the laptop, put it in the moped basket, and driven home.

Lila touched the computer and whispered, "Turn it on. I want to see it."

Proud and excited, brother fumbled around and finally found the switch. The screen lit up and the computer made a bong sound. His expression changed to fear their parents might hear.

"Let's go on the internet," Lila said.

Brother fiddled with the controls, then said, "I don't think we can do that here. We don't have wireless. We need to plug it in by the phone."

They heard a knock on the door, then it opened. Their parents stood there. "Where did you get that?" father asked.

Brother was silent.

"You stole it," father said. "My son is a thief."

"He didn't steal it," Lila said, "he took it back. They steal from us. We make the things worth more, but they sell them and give us only a little bit of that money. The lady explained it all to me. They get rich on our stolen money, and we stay poor. Just because they own everything. So we have to take it back."

"The police don't care about all that," father said. "They'll just arrest us."

"I will hide it," brother said. "I will take it to my friend's."

"You'll get fired from your job," mother said.

"They don't know it was me. It could be anybody."

"We will see about that." Father frowned at brother but then bent down and stared at the computer, his face bright with fascination.

The mother of Lila's friend came to their

apartment and told Lila her daughter was very sick and had asked that Lila come to see her. Lila went with her on the bus to the edge of the city where many people lived in huts made of boards, plastic, and tin. The mother led Lila through narrow dirt lanes among the shanties, small and packed together. They looked like playhouses, but whole families lived there. Each one was different. Some had a wooden door, others just a curtain. Some had a glass window, others a sheet of gray plastic stretched over a hole in the wall. Some had plywood walls, others corrugated tin. Some had enough space in front for a couple of chairs or a seat from a wrecked car, others opened right onto the dirt path. Some had a motor bike in front, others a bicycle, one just a Mercedes hood ornament by the front door. Some had flowers in front, others trash. Many people cooked outside, some burning sticks, others cow patties; some set their smoke-blackened pots on metal frames over the fire, others on bricks beside the fire. Some sang or talked as they cooked, others just stared. An old man swept the path with a twig broom. A little girl and her littler sister squatted in their doorway, the older teaching the younger how to make a cat's cradle. A new mother held her baby in the crook of her arm, its head under her shirt to nurse. Lila imagined her friend's mother having her baby here. Inside one of the huts a woman was chanting prayers. Something was flowing through the ditch beside the path, but it didn't seem like water. Lila was afraid someone would grab her and make her spend the rest of her life here.

The friend's hut had walls of different sized boards, a tin roof, and a mosquito net for a door. Inside was one low-ceilinged room dimly lit through plastic windows. Two hammocks were stretched between the walls. The back wall was a piece of a canvas tent. It didn't smell very good here, like a pit toilet.

Her friend was lying under blankets on the cardboard-covered floor. Her face was red and damp, but she smiled seeing Lila. She had gotten sick from the water, she said. They got their water from a pump down the lane, but it wasn't very clean. They boiled the water they drank, but they didn't know you needed to do that for the water you brush your teeth with too. The whole family had become sick, but her parents had gotten better in a few days. She had gotten worse, though. Now she had a fever, her whole body hurt, and she trembled. Lila sat beside her and held her hot, moist hand, and they cried together for a while. *If she gets hotter and hotter, what will happen to her? Will she cook inside...and die?*

The mother sat nearby on a pillow on the floor next to a big box full of blouses she was embroidering as fast as she could, the same red flower over and over. A small kerosene lamp next to her gave enough light to see to work, but it made the room smoky. The friend had helped before, but now she was too sick.

The mother said the friend was tired now. Lila patted her hand and said she would come to see her again.

Brother came home early from work, before the family went to bed. His hair was messed up, he had a bruise on his cheek, and his eyes were red. With head hanging down he told them in a mumbling voice how the whole cleaning crew had been brought into the security office, where the officer said something had been stolen and they all had to take a lie detector test. Some of the men didn't want to take the test, saying those machines weren't always accurate, but the officer said anyone who didn't take it would be fired, so they said OK. Everyone except brother. He was afraid the machine would show he was lying, and then he'd be put in jail. Getting fired would be better than jail.

He told them he hadn't stolen anything, he just didn't want to take the test because he didn't trust those machines. They told him they would search his home. He said go ahead, you won't find anything because he hadn't taken anything. They told him he was fired. Three men grabbed him, hit him, and held him while the officer took his picture, searched him, and cut off some of his hair. Then they pushed him out the gate and told him he wouldn't get paid anything and no other company would hire him now.

As brother told the story, father's frown turned into an angry scowl. "They know you are my son. I may get fired too. You have endangered our whole family." He shook his finger at him. "Now you are on the bad list and won't get another job. All that for a machine we don't even need."

Brother said he was sorry and started to cry.

"Where is the computer?" father asked. "I will give it back. Then they may not fire me."

"At my friend's."

"Go get it now."

Brother went up two floors to where the friend lived and came back with the computer. "I just wanted to be on the internet like everybody else," he said.

"In jail they don't have internet," father said.

Lila's friend came to visit. She was still weak from being sick, but her fever and pain were gone. Now her face was pale instead of red. Lila was very glad to see her, even though the friend couldn't really play.

They talked a lot, though, and Lila tried to keep it on happy things. She told about the farm and the animals. Her friend told about how her family went to the ocean once and how beautiful it was. You could run on the sandy beach and jump into the waves. The friend had learned to swim there and even had goggles to see under water: fish, rocks, swaying seaweed.

That sounded wonderful, Lila said. She had splashed in her pond, but her parents didn't know how to swim, so they couldn't teach her.

Then the friend said she needed to tell her something sad. Her father had stolen some food from a store and was in jail. Now they had even less chance of getting out of the shanties.

Hearing this, Lila got mad. "They are the thieves, not your father."

"How do you mean?" the friend asked.

"They have stolen your father, taken him away from you. They have stolen your home. And when we try to steal back, they put us in jail."

"What can we do?" the friend asked.

"I don't know," Lila said. "But we need to do something."

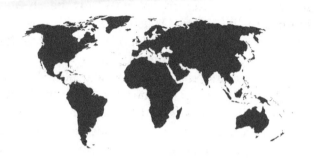

Brother proudly announced to the family he'd gotten a new job. Since he was on the bad list, though, he had to do it under another name.

Father asked if the company hadn't looked at his ID card.

Brother said they did, but he'd gotten one with another name.

Father wanted to know how he paid for it.

A friend loaned him the money, brother said, and he would pay him back from his wages. He was on the night cleaning crew of a company that weaved cloth.

"Don't steal anything this time...or do anything wrong," father said.

"I won't. I promise."

That night when they were alone brother asked Lila if she could keep a secret. She liked secrets, so she said yes. Looking ashamed, brother told her he hadn't borrowed the money from a friend. He didn't have any friends who had any money. He got it by letting a man play with his body. He didn't like to do that, but he needed the ID card or else he'd never get another job and would always feel bad for not helping the family.

Lila was glad he told her this because it showed he trusted her. But she hoped she never needed money so bad that she had to let a man play with her body.

Father showed the family a newspaper he'd bought. On the front page was a picture of burning trucks and a story about a fire at a company that sold the new kinds of seeds, fertilizers, and bug killers. Someone had set their trucks afire. "That's the company that killed grandpa," he said. "They lied about how much corn the seeds would bring, so then he couldn't pay the bank. It must've happened to other people too, and now someone took revenge. Serves them right!"

He tossed the newspaper down, saying, "That's the good news...but here's the bad news." He held up a letter he'd gotten. "The building owners are raising our rent. Now we have to pay more every month just to live in this little dump."

Mother closed her eyes a moment, and her face pinched together. "How can we get the money? They are squeezing us. The building owners raise our rent, but the factory owners don't raise our pay."

51

"Will they throw us out?" Lila asked.

"They will if we don't pay more," father said.

"Then will we have to move to the shanties?" she wanted to know.

"No, we still have our jobs, so we could move to another apartment," father said. "But it would be even smaller than this."

Lila stared up at her parents. "What if we lose our jobs too?"

"Don't think about it," mother said.

But Lila couldn't help but think about it, and the thoughts whirled into a blur like a dust storm blowing her away. Eyes wide, mouth open, she breathed in little bursts and chewed her fingernails.

Sunday afternoon mother cooked a big dinner, and Lila helped with cutting vegetables. Usually they had to eat in a hurry and they weren't all together because of different schedules, but Sundays were different. Everyone was there and they weren't rushed. Today they had chicken, and Lila wondered if it was maybe one of theirs that they had to buy back at the market.

As they were starting to eat, the doorbell rang. Father looked through the peephole to make sure it wasn't robbers and then opened the door. Five policemen stood in the hall. One of them said they had an arrest warrant for brother, who was sitting at the table looking like he wanted to run away. They made him stand up, handcuffed him, searched him, and led him out the door. Neighbors were peering out curiously.

As soon as the door was shut, father hit it with his fist. "I knew something like this would happen." He turned to mother. "He's like your brother, always a hothead. Now he's a disgrace!"

Mother cried.

Next day she found out where he was in jail, and in the evening she and Lila went to visit him. Father was too angry and stayed home. The jail was noisy and dirty, and the people working there were not friendly. A lady guard searched mother and Lila, led them into the visiting room, and told them to sit on chairs in front of a wire screen. A door on the other side of the screen opened, and brother was led in by a male guard. He smiled when he saw them, but as he sat down his mouth sagged and his forehead wrinkled. His eyes were red. "Send me to prison...a long time," he mumbled.

Mother moaned. "What did you do?"

"I set the fire at the seed company. For what they and the bank did to grandpa...and how it has ruined our lives too. I could not stand to see them just keeping on with their business, doing it to other people."

"You should not say this," mother whispered quickly.

"I already signed a paper about it. They said if I did, they would go easy on me. And you would not have to pay a lawyer. I could save you that money."

"How did you do it?" Lila wanted to know.

Brother's face became more animated. "Their warehouse was near where I worked, trucks parked behind a big fence, all locked in. When I got off work, middle of the night, I poured gasoline under the fence until it ran under the trucks. Then set fire to it. The gasoline burned, then the trucks, one after the other...each one exploding in a fireball. A guard ran out from the building, I spat at him, told him he should not work for such a company, and ran away. I had my face covered so he couldn't see me, but they found out it was me through the spit. I wish I hadn't spat." His expression grew morose again. "I will go to prison, and you can forget your bad son. Please forgive me for bringing shame on the family. And Lila, I'm sorry I hit you and was mean to you when we moved here."

"Thank you for saying you're sorry," she said. "Everything was so terrible then...and still is." *I may never see my brother again. They have taken him away...another thing they've stolen from us.* She pressed her hand against his through the wire screen.

Mother was crying but brother didn't cry. *Maybe he doesn't have any tears left*, Lila thought.

Next evening the doorbell rang. "Not the police again," father said wearily.

Instead of the police, it turned out to be a woman from the local socialist party. She told them people in the whole country had heard about what brother did, and many were glad he'd fought back against the company. Many would like to do what he had done but are too afraid. She and the other socialists wanted to organize demonstrations to convince the government not to send a sixteen-year-old boy to prison for many years. The first demo would be when brother went before a judge for his preliminary hearing.

Father argued that a demonstration might make the government go harder on him. The socialist said no, she had seen many times when the government backed down if the people got really angry. She would like the parents to speak at the demo to tell about brother and why he had done this. The woman was friendly but serious, and as she talked, her dark eyes met all of theirs. Her build was stocky and solid. Some of her hair was gray but she didn't look old.

Father was worried about losing his job, but mother convinced him their son's life was more important, they needed to speak.

The demo was in a park across from the courthouse where brother was appearing before the judge. Lila had never been in this part of town before. Office towers twice as tall as their apartment building filled the sky. Sunlight could reach the ground only in a few places. The sidewalks and streets were crowded with people and cars, and the people could walk faster than the cars could drive.

A thousand people came to the demo, many of them holding signs demanding that brother be freed and the company leaves their country. They chanted that the president of the company should be in jail, not brother. Forty police were standing around the edges of the park, some taking pictures, but they didn't come in.

The family sat on a platform with the socialist woman, who talked through a megaphone about how burning trucks is only a minor crime compared to what the companies and banks are doing to the people. Father told what had happened to them and said brother wasn't a violent criminal but had just lost his temper because of what that company had done. Mother thanked everyone for coming and hoped they could convince the government not to smash his life.

As mother gave the megaphone back to the socialist, Lila said, "I want to talk."

Mother gestured to her *no*, but the socialist said, "Let her," and gave her the megaphone. "Just hold it like this and talk right into it."

Lila walked nervously around the platform, and some people chuckled about the little girl. "They stole my brother!" she said suddenly. "I was there. They came in with guns and took him away from us. They may keep him forever and never give him back. They stole my grandpa too. They made him hang himself because he couldn't pay back the money. He had to borrow money to buy the seeds, but the seeds didn't work, so he couldn't pay back the money. They took his house and land, all we had to stay alive. They killed my grandpa. Then we had to leave our farm and move in here to a little apartment and all of us work all day long in these bad places to get enough money just to live.

"And they're stealing our money when we work. What we do makes the things worth a lot. But they only give us a little of that, just enough to keep us alive so we can keep working and they can keep stealing the money we make. They're robbing all of us, but if we rob, they put us in jail."

People in the park started cheering and shouting, "She's right!" "They're thieves!"

Lila continued, "If we don't stop them, we're all going to end up like my grandpa. They're stealing our lives. We have to stop them."

"Yes!" someone yelled. "Enough!" "Fight back!" answered others.

"We have to take our lives back from them," Lila said.

"They're killing us!" someone shouted.

"Let's start by taking my brother back. Please! Otherwise I may never see him again. He was just trying to stop the company that killed my grandpa, to keep them from killing the rest of us. They should be in jail, not my brother. Please take him back. He's in the building now. We are so many, they are so few. Please, take him!"

People were shaking their fists and shouting, "Free him!" "Break him out!" "Get him now!"

The socialist picked Lila up, held her high, and shouted, "Listen to this little girl! She's right. We can do it! They take the prisoners out the back door of the courthouse. There's our best chance to get him."

"Let's go!" Lila yelled, waving her arm towards the courthouse. With shouts of "Yes!" "Grab him!" "He's ours!" the crowd surged out of the park with Lila at the front riding on her father's shoulders. They all began to run, and he held tight to her legs so she wouldn't fall off. "You convinced me," he called up to her, and she patted him on his bouncing head. She was bouncing too, her wavy brown hair and coral necklace fluttering.

The police who had been watching were too few to stop them. All they could do was run along with them. One stayed behind, talking frantically on his cell phone, face sweaty. By the time the crowd reached the driveway leading up to the back of the courthouse, a line of cops was blocking it, arms linked. The chief cop stood in front holding a megaphone in one hand and a club in the other. Behind them all, at the rear door, stood a police car with a dozen cops around it.

"Turn around and go back! Clear the street!" the chief bellowed through the megaphone to the people.

The police car pulled away from the courthouse and drove slowly down the driveway surrounded by police.

"He's in the back!" Lila shouted. "I see him."

A cheer went up from the crowd. "Block the car!" someone shouted, and the crowd streamed forward.

"Use your clubs!" the chief commanded his troops, then charged the first person approaching. As the man raised his arms to defend himself, the cop swung his club into the corner of his neck and shoulder. With a scream the man collapsed to the ground. "That's how you do it!" the chief shouted, club held high. He started to swing it again at the man on the ground, but two women pushed him, and he staggered sideways. The man on the ground managed to grab the chief's leg and twist. The women pushed him again, he toppled over, they began kicking him.

Half the cops ran to help their chief, leaving gaps in the police line through which the people ran. The cops around the car put on gas masks and began hurling tear gas grenades into the approaching crowd. One landed near Lila and her father, spinning and spouting a gray cloud. They began coughing, and father doubled over as the fumes hit his lungs. Lila fell off his shoulders and sprawled onto the ground crying. Father picked up the grenade and threw it back towards the car with a cry of pain, then blew and spat on his fingers, burned red from the hot grenade. "Are you OK?" he asked Lila. Eyes seared, nose and throat raw, skin burning, she couldn't answer. Her knees were bleeding. The beads of her coral necklace were scattered on the street.

Other people began throwing grenades back, using hats or handkerchiefs to protect their hands. As gas enveloped the car, the driver, who wasn't wearing a gas mask, tried to bull his way through the crowd to get away. He hit a woman and she went down under the wheels screaming.

Enraged, people began pounding and kicking the car windows. One man leaped onto the hood, smashed the windshield with a rock, and smashed the rock into the driver's face. The car stopped.

People were attacking the police in their midst and ripping their gas masks off. One cop pulled out his pistol but began coughing too convulsively to aim it. Two men grabbed him from behind; a third wrenched the pistol from his hands; the others beat him to the ground.

The man who took the pistol pointed it into the police car and said, "Out!"

The doors opened and guards emerged staggering and coughing, hair sparkling with glass diamonds from the shattered window. Brother was still on the back seat, arms and legs chained. "Take him!" Lila called in a hoarse, raw voice.

They dragged brother from the car, and four men, one for each limb, carried him in the midst of the protective crowd as they ran from the courthouse. Some cops managed to grab a few people, but the rest ran faster and got away.

"Go down this street," a woman shouted. "My car's there." They ran to it, and she opened the doors. Mother kissed brother on the cheek, they put him in the back of the car, he waved an astonished farewell with his chained hands, and the woman drove away with him as the crowd cheered. Sirens wailed as police reinforcements arrived.

Lila clambered onto the hood of a parked car, staggered getting her balance, and then rasped, tears streaming from her brown eyes, "My brother is free! Thank you! Thank you!"

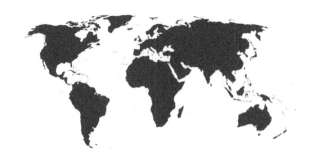

Next morning as Lila was lacing shoes, the floor lady, the personnel chief, and a policewoman walked up to her table. "Come with us," said the floor lady. They went downstairs to an office where father was sitting with a policeman. Father looked too worried to smile at her.

"You both have been summoned to the juvenile counseling center," the personnel chief told them. "Depending on the outcome of that, you may or may not be further employed here. Go with the officers now."

The police searched them, and Lila didn't like how the lady touched her. *Does she think I have a gun?* They put them in the back of a car that had steel mesh dividing the back from the front. It reminded her of the screen that had divided them from brother at the jail. *Where is he now?*

They drove downtown near the courthouse. She hoped he was someplace safe where people were taking care of him. She hoped they had got the chains off him. How would they do that?

They parked in an underground garage, and the police led them into an elevator and then through a long hall to an office where mother sat in a chair with a policewoman standing behind her. Mother nodded to them, lips together. A woman in a dark suit sat behind a large desk in front of the flags of the state and country. The police told them to sit in the two chairs next to mother, and they stood behind them. The woman smiled at them out of a thin face with silver-rimmed rectangular glasses.

"Don't worry," she told them. "This is not a court but a family counseling session. Sometimes families get into problems and need counseling. The most important thing is to protect the children and see that they are safe and in a good environment."

She looked at some papers on her desk and said that some disturbing facts had come to her attention. Lila had apparently made some inflammatory remarks to a crowd of people that had inspired them to attack police officers, damage a police vehicle, and forcibly remove a criminal suspect from custody. Was this true?

Lila said that the police had stolen her brother, and she had asked the people to take him back.

The counselor wanted to know where Lila got the idea her brother had been stolen.

"I was there," she said. "They came in and took him."

"Who took him?"

"The police."

"But, Lila, who told you that is stealing? The police just needed to ask him some questions."

"But they wouldn't give him back."

"But your brother confessed to a very serious crime. They can't just give him back. You're a good girl, but sometimes you do something wrong and need to be punished, right?" The counselor looked at her inquiringly.

Lila said nothing.

"Well, it's the same with your brother. He needs to have some punishment to learn not to do things like that. Then the police will give him back. But he first needs to learn his lesson so he doesn't do it again. I'm sure a smart girl like you can understand that."

Mother and father were looking increasingly worried.

"It's good you love your brother and want to see him again, but you said some very dangerous things, some wrong things. And it was wrong of your parents to put those wrong things in your head. I'm sure your parents just wanted to get their son free, they didn't really want to hurt anybody, but they shouldn't have given you those dangerous ideas." The counselor stared at mother and father. "They weren't good parents to do that.

And until they learn to be good parents, we can't let you be with them. Bad parents aren't good for children. So for the time being we are going to put you, Lila, in another home with good parents and lots of brothers and sisters. Then later, when they learn their lesson, you can be back with your parents. And when your brother learns his lesson, the whole family can be back together and not do wrong things.

"Lila, I'm remanding you to the care of the district children's home. And for the parents" — she leaned towards them and tapped her finger on the desk — "I need to tell you that being a parent is a serious responsibility and you have failed both of your children in that. I'm forbidding you contact with them until you have successfully completed counseling sessions here at the family center and are deemed to be responsible parents.

"You must sign these documents."

The district children's home was a big building with a playground behind it, all surrounded by a high fence. The bottom floor was administration, the second floor for girls, the top for boys. Six children lived in each small room with three double-deck bunks and six metal lockers for their clothes. The windows were covered with steel mesh like in the jail and police car. The children were between six and twelve years old, most of them there for stealing. The first night Lila cried herself to sleep; so did most of the other girls in the room.

During the day, though, it was better than at the factory. In the mornings they had three hours of lessons, so they weren't as tired and could learn. In the afternoons they had to work, but only three hours compared to four in the factory. It wasn't called work but rehabilitation, so they got less money per hour. Lila was assigned to numerical skills: counting screws and putting them into plastic boxes. Each box had six sections for different kinds of screws, and she had to put ten screws of the right kind into each section, then tape the box closed. A lady came around to check them, but she was friendlier than the lady at the shoe factory. Lila liked this work better because the metal didn't give her a rash like the shoes did.

They had forty-five minutes morning and afternoon to run around and play, and she didn't have to wait as long as in the park to get a free swing. The seesaws worked. There was a volleyball court with a lower net, and she learned how to play that. And she played soccer. At night they had TV and DVDs. The food didn't taste as good as what mother cooked, but you could have all you wanted. Always you had to stay inside the fence, a high fence with barbed wire.

She kept wondering how her parents and brother were doing and when she would see them again. At least brother was free, or at least she hoped he was still free. That made being here not so bad. She had done something important. And she liked that.

A few days later the matron told her she had visitors and took her to the family room. Her father and the socialist woman were there with big smiles: Lila could come home. The socialists' lawyer had gone to court and argued that freedom of speech applied to children too and the family counselor had no proof that mother and father were bad parents. The court had overturned the counselor's ruling.

Father hugged her with happy tears in his eyes, and they packed up her things. She said good-bye to the other girls, some of whom cried in envy.

As they waited for the bus, the socialist woman showed Lila newspapers with brother's picture and stories about the escape of a dangerous criminal and a reward for his capture. She told Lila he was in another city now, hiding with comrades there.

Lila asked if he got his chains off.

Yes, she explained, they got a special saw that could cut through metal. She told Lila her speech had inspired people in a way she had never seen before. It made them realize they weren't helpless, they really could change things.

Father said he was proud of her for saving

her brother. He could now see that we needed to fight the owners and the government, even if that made things worse for us for a while. There was no other way out.

"Lila," the woman told her, "we have socialists all over the world working for change, but they need a spark to unite them, bring them together. I think you could be that spark."

"Good," she said. "I like sparks."

The socialists called another meeting in the park, and many more people came this time. Many more police came too, standing around the edges in helmets and bullet-proof vests with clubs, gas masks, and stun guns at the ready. The driveway to the court house was blocked by a mass of police and two trucks with high-pressure water hoses.

"My brother isn't inside. Why do they block it?" Lila asked.

"They have to make a show of force," the socialist woman said. "They always overreact but too late. We're off to something new, and they're one step behind us. That's our advantage over them. Their advantage over us, though, is they're so brutal."

"They ran over that lady with their car," Lila said. "Did they kill her?"

"No, she's still alive."

"I'm glad."

"So is she."

A helicopter buzzed above like an angry bee as Lila, the socialist, and her parents walked through the crowd in the park. Many people pointed to Lila and smiled; some wanted to shake her hand. The socialist stood up on park bench with her megaphone and said, "Welcome, everyone! The city banned our demo and wouldn't let us put up a platform, so we'll use the bench. They won't let us march, either, and this time they have enough cops to enforce it. The plain fact is they're scared, scared of you, scared of the people. The people are starting to rise up, and the owners are determined to push us back down. They have to push us back down, or else they'll lose their power and the money they take from us.

"This week our rising up has reached a new level, and so has their repression." She motioned to Lila, who hopped up on the bench. "They took this little girl away from her parents and locked her up so she couldn't talk to you. But we got her out. We got her brother out, too. But with Lila we did it legally. Even their own court said it was wrong to lock her up. So she's here today to inspire us to rise up even higher. Lila, talk to us." She gave her the megaphone while the crowd cheered.

Lila didn't know what to say, so she just started talking. "Our friends cut my brother's chains off. But he's not really free because he still has to hide. They're looking all over the country for him." She got more enthused and talked louder.

"We're not really free, either. We belong to the company. We have to work for whatever they pay us. Our work makes lots of money for them, but instead of giving it to us, they keep most of it for themselves and give us enough to barely live on." The bench wasn't big enough for her to pace around, but she stepped back and forth and waved her finger as she spoke.

"My brother stole a computer once and got fired from his job and put on the bad list. But they steal from us all the time. Our work makes them rich.

"This morning I could see we don't need them. What do they do? They just own what we make.

"We took my brother back from them. Now we need to take ourselves back from them...and what we made. We made the buildings, the machines, all the things they sell. If we don't take them back, we'll always be their slaves.

"I could see this morning how they trick us. When we're there at work, we have the factory. But when we leave, they take it back from us. It's theirs again. But if enough of us don't leave, we can keep it as ours. Half of us go home and half stay to keep the factory. Then the next day we trade. So one night we sleep at home and the next night sleep in the factory. Bring enough food. We sell the things we make and divide up the money, everybody gets the same. We'll have a lot more than now. And we can have insurance and decide how fast we want to work. We don't need them."

Most people applauded, but a man in front shouted, "It's useless! The cops will just force us out. They'll arrest us and give us fines. The company will fire us. We'll be worse off than before."

Lila tossed her head to get the hair out of her eyes. "If they throw us out from one place, we go to another place. They can't throw us out from everywhere. Look how many we are compared to them. And they can't fire us because it's our company now."

The socialist motioned to Lila that she wanted to talk, and Lila gave her the megaphone. "Occupying the factories is a great idea. If you get a fine, we have a fund that will pay it," the woman spoke. "All of us who've been in this struggle know that sooner or later we're going to have to fight them, to take the factories, the corporations, the banks, the resources back from those people who have been forcing us to live such desperate lives. We need to work for ourselves, not for them. We can't be sure we'll win this time, but should we try?"

Most people shouted "Yes!," shook their

fists, and stamped the ground. But some called out, "No, they'll crush us!" "It's too dangerous."

"What we have now is dangerous!" the socialist responded. "Look at how we live. We're all prisoners. It's time to fight for our freedom."

The crowd cheered.

"I've been organizing workers for twenty years to get to this point. And now we're ready," she continued. "We'll meet now in factory groups to plan it."

One woman called out, "My factory runs twenty-four hours a day. How do we handle that?"

"We'll work that out in the groups," the socialist said. "I have a surprise for you now." She handed the megaphone down to a woman in front who was sitting in a wheelchair.

The woman took it and said, "Most of you can't see me now because I can't stand up. The reason for that is I have two broken legs from a police car that ran over me. I have to be in a cast for a couple of months. So I can't take over my factory. But I'll help how I can. Now is the time to fight back. We can't let them keep rolling over us and breaking our lives. We have to stop them. And thank you, Lila. You're the one who's made us see we can do it. We're not sure exactly what will happen, but we'll start and see."

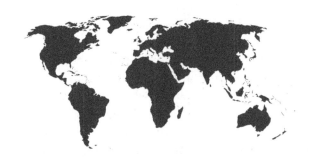

Mother invited Lila's friend and her mother to visit on Sunday for an afternoon of cooking. Lila had told her how hard it was to cook in the huts, so mother had the idea they could cook here once a week. They arrived with bags of food, especially flour, because the plan was to bake three loaves of bread and take them back.

The friend was almost all better now. Her smile had returned and her skin was again a healthy tan. The mothers did most of the work, but the girls helped with kneading the dough, forming it into loaves, and sliding them into the oven. While the bread baked, they helped make dinner on the stove: washing the rice and lentils, slicing potatoes, boiling water for tea. Father said it smelled great and asked if he could help, but mother kissed him on the cheek and shooed him out, saying he'd just be in the way.

During the next week the people organized their

co-workers in the factories. Only about half were willing to join the takeback; the rest were too afraid. Each day the determined ones sneaked in a few more supplies and stored them in their lockers. They met after work to make plans, but they told their colleagues who didn't want to join them that they had abandoned the idea. They coordinated with the other factories and picked a day to all start together, so the police would be spread thin.

Finally they were ready. They worked their shift that day in hopeful, fearful excitement, exchanging hard smiles and conspiratorial glances. When the bell rang ending their shift, they all stood and shouted in unison: "This factory belongs to us. We built it, we run it, it's ours! We're taking it back! Join us now or get out of the way."

Lila did this with some of the other children in the shoe-lacing section, then they ran to be with their parent who worked in the factory. The halls were full of running, shouting people: angry supervisors and security officers, fearful workers trying to get out. As Lila reached her father's department, the floor leader was checking off names on his employee roster. He told them all they had five minutes to leave or else they would be fired and bad listed.

Her father shouted at him, "You're fired right now! We're the new owners. Get out of here!"

"You're all fools!" the floor leader shouted back. "We knew your plans. The cops are downstairs right now. We're emptying out your lockers. Your little game is over...unless you leave right now. I'll give you one more chance."

The group exchanged anxious glances, then four men walked away, eyes downcast to avoid contact with the others.

"You men are smart," the floor leader told them, unchecking their names from the list. "In about five minutes the rest of you are going to wish you'd joined them."

He swaggered out, and the workers grimaced. Finally one said, "For better or worse, we're staying."

"Yes!" said another. "We never thought it would be easy. We have to stick together no matter what."

And another, "We're glad to have you with us, Lila."

She smiled and said, "I know we will win."

From the floor below they heard shouts and a few screams. Boots stomped up their stairway. Three cops appeared in the door. In their gas masks they looked like monsters, and Lila wanted to run away. But she didn't. She held father's hand tighter. "Get out or get gassed," a cop said. Through the mask he sounded like a duck. One cop plugged a big fan into the wall and set it in the doorway pointing into the room. Another pulled the pins on two tear gas grenades and tossed them in front of the fan. The grenades spun around on the floor, spewing toxic fumes, and the workers ran away towards the back stairwell. At the first whiff Lila's throat tightened and her eyes stung like someone was pouring acid into them. Father picked her up and ran with her, both of them coughing and crying. "Not the stairs," Lila said. "Go in there." She pointed to the door into the management section. "They won't be in there."

This door was always locked and only managements had keys, but father set Lila down and with two kicks broke it open. Other workers ran in with them and pulled it shut. The air was instantly better, and they gulped it down while staring curiously at the carpeted floors, comfortable chairs, neat desks, and pictures on the walls. "Let's take things," Lila said. She saw a laptop computer on a desk and lifted it with both hands. The others grabbed whatever looked valuable and portable. Father got a calculator and traded Lila the heavier computer.

"Let's burn the place down," one man said.

"No," Lila said, "it's ours. We don't want to burn it down. We want to take it back."

They ran down the management staircase. A security guard stood blocking the door, shouting at them to stop. One of the men ran at him and smashed his fist into his face, kicked him, knocked him down; the others ran over him into the fresh air.

Outside people were running every which way, coughing from gas and cursing the cops, who were mostly over by the workers' entrance grabbing and arresting as many people as they could as they staggered out the door. Off to the side a man knelt on the ground giving mouth-to-mouth resuscitation to a boy Lila knew from the lacing and lessons. She and father ran the other way from the cops but saw they and several other workers were trapped inside the fence. If they had to go out through the gate, they'd get arrested and lose their stuff.

The chain-link fence was three meters tall and topped with barbed wire. The fence posts were set in concrete, and the chain-links were held to them by twisted loops of wire. "It's too solid," father said. But then he saw a pile of iron rods on the ground. He took a rod and poked it through the bottom wire loop on the fence, then pushed on it with all his strength. With a metallic squeal it loosened.

He untwisted two more wires, then could push the bottom of the fence enough to raise it a bit. Lila and a thin woman squirmed their way under it. They helped hold it up from the outside, and a thin man wriggled under. The chain-links were easier to lift up from the outside than to push up from the inside, so the three of them were able to hold it up long enough for the others to scramble through.

They ran, still weeping from tear gas but also now laughing from their escape. Staying off the main street where the police might be, they made their way to a farther bus stop, where they could blend in. They'd been defeated but they were still free. They were in the mood for a fight.

"I thought we would win. But we lost." Lila stared forlornly up at her father, then her face brightened. "But we got a computer! Show me the internet."

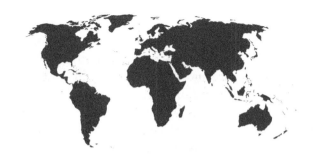

"Yes, they won this time," the socialist woman told a meeting of workers in the park, voice sluggish with discouragement. "We got driven out of every factory, many of us arrested. We weren't expecting so many police. They brought in cops from three other cities.

"But the worst is, a boy died of an asthma attack. Ten years old. He'd had asthma for a long time, and this was too much for him. His lungs filled with fluid and shut down. The cops know it's dangerous to use tear gas indoors, but they did it anyway. They killed him." She thrust her arms out and opened her hands. "We're going to sue them for wrongful death and try to get a ban on using it indoors."

A shocked murmur rose from the crowd. *The boy on the ground*, thought Lila. *Oh no! A nice boy. Dead. Like grandpa. My fault. If I hadn't told the people to do this, he'd still be alive. But now it's too late. No way to bring him back.*

"This whole thing was a disaster," shouted a woman in the crowd. "That family lost their son, and most of us have lost our jobs. The owners are hiring new workers. We're on the bad list now, so no one will hire us. We can't pay our rent. We'll get evicted and end up in the shanties."

Lila imagined everyone here moving into huts like her friend's family did. Her fault. A black shroud seemed to fall over her, shutting out air and light. She wanted to disappear into it.

But then the owners would win and things would stay the way they were. She didn't want that. That would be worse than the black shroud. There had to be something else they could do. Together. Her friend's family had been all alone. Maybe that was the trouble. As Lila thought about what had happened to them and to her family and to the boy and to the whole group here, she got mad. She didn't want to disappear. She wanted to make the owners disappear.

Lila shuffled from one foot to the other on the park bench, tugged on the socialist's sleeve, and pointed to the megaphone. The woman gave it to her, and she spoke to the group, "I saw how the owners threw out my friend's family. Men came in and carried their furniture out and set it on the street. The family was only three people, so they couldn't stop the men. But if a lot of people had been there, the men couldn't have come in.

"Now that we all don't have go to our jobs,

we can help each other. If somebody's going to be thrown out, we all go there. We fill the place up."

"No," someone shouted, "the cops will just pull us out one by one."

Lila thought for a moment and said, "We'll get chains like they put on my brother. We'll chain us all together and chain ourselves to the furniture. The refrigerator! If we're all chained to the refrigerator, they can't move all that. And the stove...the bed...everything together, they can't throw us out."

"They'll tear gas us," someone called out.

What if someone else dies? Lila thought. *My fault.* The black shroud started to fall over her again, but she shook herself to push it away. *We can't quit. We need to keep trying.* "No one who's sick should be there. Only healthy people," she said. "And we'll get those masks like the police have. Can we get those masks?" she asked the socialist.

The woman took the megaphone back and spoke to the group. "I'll see about getting gas masks. There's lots of things we can do to fight evictions. We're learning to struggle together and defend ourselves. We've got some emergency funds to start a food bank, so no one's going to starve, at least."

"Can you pay our rent?" a woman with a bandaged head asked.

"No, we can't," the socialist admitted with a

regretful shrug. "I wish we could."

As she spoke, several trucks pulled up around the edges of the park and police began jumping out. A loudspeaker on one of the trucks blared: "Clear the park! Court order. Gatherings of more than twelve people are now prohibited. Leave the grounds immediately."

"Recognize that voice?" the socialist asked the group. "That's the chief who clubbed the man down at our first demo. The people defeated him, and now he's hiding in a truck. And the courts ban our meetings—that means they're afraid of us. If we stay together, we can win this fight! But not today."

Lines of cops began advancing on the group from three edges of the park, clubs drawn. Some people began to run.

"Our meetings are going to have to go virtual," she said hurriedly. "We're going to post a chat room on the socialist website, so we can keep communicating. We'll make announcements there, and you can let everyone know what's happening." As the cops approached, the group dissolved into fleeing individuals. "For now, though, we run away to fight another day. Let's get out of here."

Lila's friend and the mother came again to cook and visit. The friend had her full energy back, and she taught Lila tricks. Lila could already do simple jump-roping, but the friend knew the fancy stuff. She could do double bounces, where you jumped twice for each swing of the rope, jumping fast and swinging slow; and double unders, where you swing twice for each jump, swinging fast while trying to hang in the air. She taught Lila how to count while doing them, which made it easier.

The friend could do gymnastic tricks: somersaults, handstands, and cartwheels. These were hard, and Lila often fell, but she liked them and kept trying until she got pretty good. They did a show for the grownups, who thought they were great.

Lila noticed her parents were holding hands as they watched. She was happy that they were more friendly now.

Lila stood with her parents, the socialist woman, and two hundred workers in front of forty police guarding the gate to her mother's sewing factory. Lila was wearing rubber sandals, purple shorts, and a yellow T-shirt that looked good with her dark-brown eyes and hair and tan skin. She knew there would probably be a fight today, and she had the feeling they would win. But she didn't trust it because she'd had that feeling the last time, and she'd been wrong. She was definitely going to try to win, though.

The socialist handed the megaphone to Lila's mother and said, "We need to convince the people inside to stop work and join us. And you can do that better than I can. To them, I'm just a socialist agitator, and they've heard so much propaganda about how terrible socialism is. But they know you. They're open to what you have to say."

"I'll try," mother said. She blew into the

megaphone to test it, and then called through it, "My friends inside. Most of you know me, and we've worked together. But our work has made the owners rich and kept us poor. Now we need to work together to fight for a decent life for our families. At this point the only way to do that is to shut the factory down. Then the owners will have to negotiate with us. They'll have to give us better pay, give us accident insurance and safer conditions. But if you keep making clothes, they'll never change. We've got to close them down. I ask you to stop working right now, walk out the gate, and join us. Together we can win. We've got a food bank, so we'll all eat. If they try to evict us from our apartments, we'll fight them together. It's time to take a stand...or they'll keep on owning us...and everything else too.

"We heard there's a bus full of scabs on the way here now to break the strike. Our first job is to stop them."

Mother gave the megaphone to Lila. "Now you try."

This is my gun, Lila thought as she held it up and said, "I don't work in your factory, I work in another one. But I know you have children working here. They fold the clothes and bring the sewers more thread. And you have people like my mother sewing clothes, putting their life into machines that take their fingers.

"If we put our lives into the machines, they

87

are really ours. Those people just say they own them. But if you keep working for them, you'll belong to them—their slave. That's all you'll ever be. Turn off your machines, come outside, join us. We're all in this together. If we really want it, we can win."

The workers around her began chanting, "Join us! Join us!"

Some workers inside applauded and waved their hands from the windows, open in the afternoon heat. Then shouts came from inside the factory, and the windows banged shut. A minute later, though, the main doors opened and fifty people streamed out. They gathered in front of the gate and demanded to be let out.

The two groups of workers embraced as they met. "We should've come sooner," the newcomers said. "The important thing is you're here," the oldtimers replied. Those from inside said they were forced to work fourteen-hour shifts but the company still couldn't produce enough to fill the orders. Half the machines were standing empty.

"See, we do have power," the socialist said. "Now more than half the workers have joined the strike."

A bus turned on to their road and drove slowly towards the factory. "Uh oh, that must be the scabs, come to take our jobs," she said. "We're not going to let them."

The chief cop ordered the workers through his megaphone: "Clear the road, let the bus in, or we'll arrest you all." His troops began moving forward, brandishing their clubs.

The socialist told her troops: "Move back but stay on the road. We've got them outnumbered six to one. Don't obey them but don't provoke them."

The cops began running at them, and the workers ran back on the road towards the bus. A few got clubbed and dragged away, but the others were faster. They clogged the road in front of the bus. The driver wasn't a cop: he couldn't just run over people like the one driving the police car had done. He stopped his bus, swore, and honked the horn. The workers pulled out knives and slashed the tires. As the air whistled out, they began rocking the bus back and forth.

The cops were trying to chase the workers away by clubbing them and blasting pepper spray in their faces. One sprayed Lila's mother right in the eyes; she shrieked in pain and doubled over, clutching her face. Lila's eyes stung just from being nearby. Father kicked the cop in the side and sent him sprawling onto the road. He kept kicking him, but when the cop reached for his pistol, father dived on top of him. Another worker joined him, and they held him fast and wrenched his hand away from the holster. Father pulled out the pistol and pointed it at the cop, who stared up at him pleadingly.

"No!" Lila shouted.

"I should shoot you for what you did to my wife," father said. "Instead I'll just do it to you." He picked the pepper spray off the road and squirted it into his eyes. The cop shrieked and clutched his face. "Now get out of here."

The cop limped away, hands to his head. Father put the pistol in one jacket pocket and the pepper spray in another. Lila picked up the club and gave it to him. He stuck it through his belt. They both bent over mother.

"Water...wash my eyes," she said through tears, her face distorted with anguish. He didn't have any water, so he spat on a handkerchief and swabbed her eyes. Lila did the same and held mother's head while they both cried.

"You're all under arrest," the chief cop thundered through his megaphone. Seeing this had no effect, he pulled out his pistol and pointed it at them. "Clear the area, or I'll open fire!"

Two men who had grappled another cop to the ground now dragged him to his feet and held him with his pistol pointed at his head. "If you shoot, we shoot!" one of them shouted to the chief.

The socialist spoke to the chief through her megaphone. "We're holding him hostage until we finish. Then we'll leave...and let him go."

Red faced with rage, the chief holstered his

pistol. He and his outnumbered troops gathered defensively around the police bus that had brought them.

The socialist approached the bus that had brought the scabs. "You have to come out," she said to the people inside, who were sitting fearfully behind closed windows. "We won't hurt you. We just need to talk to you."

A window was lowered, and a man said, "We can talk from the bus."

"You are here to take our jobs away from us," the socialist said. "We won't let you do that."

"We didn't know we'd be taking someone's job," the man said. "We were just told there was work here. So we came."

"There is work here, and we can do it together. But first we have to shut the factory down so the owners will negotiate with us. If you want to join us, you can. If you don't, then leave and we won't hurt you." She knocked on the bus door. "Open up so people can get out."

The driver shook his head.

"If you don't open the door, we'll rock the bus over."

The workers started pushing it back and forth. The driver opened the door and stepped out, hands raised defensively.

"We don't have anything against you," the socialist told him. "You can go. But tell your boss, the next time he ships scabs we'll burn the bus."

Not meeting her eyes, the driver walked rapidly away, pulling out a cell phone.

"Everybody off the bus," she said.

The people got out looking apologetic, glancing anxiously around them. "We didn't know," one said placatingly.

"Do you come from the shanties?" the socialist asked.

They nodded yes.

"If there's a job, we have to take it," a woman said. "Otherwise we starve."

"If we fight together, we can change that," the socialist said.

Distant sirens were approaching. "More cops. We won this time because we outnumbered them. But we're not going to push our luck. As the Vietnamese general who defeated the Americans said, 'Knowing when to quit is half the battle.'

"We need to scatter now, but we'll meet at the shanties in an hour. And we'll talk about what we can do so everyone has a good job."

They released the hostage cop without his weapons and moved off in different directions. "Come with me," the socialist woman said to Lila's family. "We'll make plans." Father steadied mother with a supporting arm as they walked through back streets to another bus stop. "How are your eyes?" the socialist asked mother.

"Hurt...like boiling acid mixed with ashes."

"Pepper spray and tear gas are really chemical warfare the government uses against its own people. They think we're their enemy. And it's true." The socialist turned to Lila and patted her. "You're doing a great job. People really respond to you."

"I just say what I'm thinking."

"Well, I wish I could've thought that clearly when I was your age. I didn't start thinking that way until I was a teenager. I was in an orphanage then."

"How did you get in an orphanage?" Lila asked, afraid it might happen to her.

The woman grimaced at the memory. "My mother and father got killed in a fire in a factory where they worked. The company didn't want to spend money on safety equipment. The leader of the orphanage was a socialist. He had to keep his political views hidden so he could keep his job, but he taught me a lot. And he helped me get a scholarship so I could go to college."

"I'd like to get a scholarship," said Lila.

"I hope you can. Maybe I can help you."

"How did you do it?"

"Well, they make it very hard. The state government has one scholarship each year so an orphan can go to college. They have thousands of orphans but one scholarship. To win, you have to write an essay. He knew what sort of an essay the government wanted, and he helped me write it. It was about how much the government is trying to help the people. He said to survive in this world you have to lie.

"In college I learned more about socialism, the different kinds. I wanted to be a teacher, but by the time I graduated I was on the bad list for being a radical, so no school would hire me. I started working for the party and have been doing that ever since."

"It sounds like fun to work for a party," Lila said. "Like always having a birthday."

"Well, a political party isn't quite like a birthday party," the socialist said with a laugh. "It's not always fun, but it's important. And I like most of the people. Except the government sends agents in to spy on us. We don't know who they are, so we can't trust everyone. That makes it harder to work together. Their agents told them our plans to occupy the factories, so they were ready for us. They won that battle. But we have agents too. There's a cop who's actually on our side, and he told us where and when the scabs were coming. The police have to guard all the factories now, so we could concentrate our people here and outnumber them. This time we won."

"This time was better," Lila said. "Like when we freed my brother. I like winning better than losing." Her chipped tooth tattered her smile.

"So do I," said the socialist. "But the way most revolutions go is you lose, you lose, you lose, and then you win big. The Vietnamese lost every battle against the Americans but won the war."

"Speaking of war," father said, "what should I do with this?" He pulled the police pistol out of his pocket.

"Keep it," the woman said. "You may need it."

They rode the bus to shantytown, and as others arrived there from the factory battle, the socialist told them to go through the lanes and call everyone to a meeting. Lila ran through the jumble of huts to her friend's. The mother was in front squatting on the ground heating something in a tin can beside a fire of sticks. She looked more pregnant now. The friend came out, happy to see Lila.

Lila told them about the meeting and the fight to take over the factories. The mother said she hoped they would win and she'd like to help, but fighting might harm the baby. The friend wanted to come to the meeting, though, so the two of them went back.

By then a crowd had gathered on the field next to the shanties, and the socialist spoke through her megaphone: "We're all workers, whether we have jobs or not, and we need to stick together! We know recruiters are coming through here offering you jobs. They want you to be scabs, to take jobs away from other workers. The owners are trying to break our strike. They want us to fight each other instead of them. That way they can continue to keep us all poor.

"It's true that you're even poorer than the rest of us, because you don't have jobs. We at least have lousy jobs. And that split between us is essential for the owners' profits. You're the poorest of the poor, and without you, the owners wouldn't be rich. Your desperation, your need to take any job even if it's someone else's, keeps wages low for all workers. You're the anchor on the economy that holds wages down and preserves their profits. They need you...and they need to keep you poor.

"If you don't take our jobs but instead join us in the fight to take over these factories, we can all have good jobs. We'll work the factories together. The profits that are making the owners rich really belong to all of us. We know you have to live, and if you're on our side, you can share our food bank. We'll make sure your family gets enough to eat."

A man from the crowd shouted, "You're preaching communism! Godless communism! You promise us food, but you want to make us slaves to an atheist dictator. God knows what's best for us. He'll give us enough to eat if we pray to him. If He doesn't, it's because our prayers aren't sincere. You're preaching the Devil's way!

You'll send us to Hell. God will take us to Heaven!" The man was thin, wide eyed, face glistening with sweat, finger pointing skyward.

A group around him applauded, but others hooted and called out, "Crazy!"

"It's not from lack of prayer that people are starving," the socialist continued, "but from lack of money to buy food. And the money is there. It's just all piled up in a few hands, and we have to spread it around.

"One of the best ways to spread it around is to build public housing. If we gave people jobs building nice apartments, this whole area could be a fine place to live. The money for housing is there. And the money to give everyone a good job is also there. We just need to change the economy to meeting people's needs instead of making profits for the owners.

"The first step in doing that is to shut these factories down so the owners will have to meet our demands. And our demands are a good job for everyone. More pay and fewer hours, so they have to hire more people. Safer conditions so people aren't injured. And if they are injured, insurance to pay their wages until they can work again.

"You can be part of all this, and you can benefit from it. You need to throw out the scab recruiters when they come around trying to get you to break the strike. And we want you to come to the demo for public housing and no evictions that's coming up. Most of you have been evicted, so we need your advice. Now let's all meet in smaller groups and get to know one another."

"I want to help," the friend told Lila. "What can I do?"

Lila thought for a moment, thumb pressed against her chin. "Maybe we can convince the people to break your father out of jail like they did with my brother."

"That would be great," the friend said. "Please get him out. Otherwise we'll never get out of the shanties. No one will give my mother a job because the baby's coming."

"We'll do it!" Lila said.

The socialist woman had a birthday, and she invited Lila and her parents to the party. It wasn't a very good party, Lila thought. There weren't any games and only one kind of cake. It was mostly adults standing around the socialist office talking and eating little sandwiches—cheese and cucumbers—yuck! Maybe adults didn't know how to give a good party. Maybe that's something they forgot when they got old. She'd heard that old people forget things. She hoped she never got so old that she'd forget how to give a party. The socialist was forty—that was five times older than Lila. Five times! She was older even than her parents. Some of her hair was gray. But she was very nice. Next year Lila would help her plan a proper birthday party. Maybe the problem was that she'd never had children. They could've taught her. She was married once a long time ago but not anymore.

Lila thought about how she would feel if her father was locked in jail for stealing food and she could visit him only the way she had visited brother. He could never pick her up and give her a hug. And until he was out of jail and could get another job, the family would have to live in the shanties and not have enough to eat. Lila asked the socialist if they could get the friend's father out of jail like they had her brother.

"That would be very hard to do," the woman replied. "We could grab your brother because they brought him out of jail for his hearing. But your friend's father is locked deep in the jail."

Lila was disappointed. "Couldn't we break into the jail, a whole bunch of people crash in...and take him out? Take everybody out?"

The socialist shook her head. "We're not that strong. They have so many guns. If we tried to break in, they would shoot us."

"Then the family will have to stay in the shanties," Lila said dismally.

The skin around the woman's eyes creased. "I'll try to figure out some other way to get him free."

"Thank you. So will I." Lila's voice regained its determination.

A family—mother, father, three children—came into the office and seemed surprised to see a party going on. They saw the socialist and walked over to her. She looked at them with an inquiring smile, and the father, a tall man with furrowed forehead, handed her a paper and said, "We're getting evicted. And it's your fault!" His jaw protruded as he spoke. "It was your plan to take over the factories that got me fired. Without a paycheck I can't pay the rent. What are we supposed to do?" His wife and children looked on sullenly.

The socialist's smile slipped into a frown. "I'm sorry to hear that. But *we* haven't made your lives worse. The owners have. This is further proof that we have to take their power over our lives away from them. And we can do that!" She glanced at the paper and nodded. "They want to throw you out, but whether they *can* is another matter. We have a plan for blocking evictions. Were you at the last meeting in the park? It was Lila's idea. We're going to fill the apartments with people and lock ourselves on. Make it just too difficult for them to clear the apartment. And we're going to get press coverage to get people on our side. We can't guarantee it's going to work every time, but we're going to do everything we can to keep you in your home."

"I'll believe it when I see it," the man said. "Now I know why everything is so messed up here. You get your ideas from a child." He snatched the paper from her hand, and the family stalked out.

The socialist's face flushed and she sighed. "What can I do?" she said in a small voice.

"You have a very difficult job," Lila's father said. "People expect you to work miracles."

She nodded and managed a wrinkled smile.

The next time Lila's friend and her mother came to visit they baked a cake along with the loaves of bread. It was in two layers, and the girls got to ice it, spreading mango marmalade between the layers and rose petal jam on top, then licking the spreading forks clean. They also made cabbage-tomato soup and a potato omelet with chili powder.

The friend taught Lila double-dutch jump-roping. This had to be out in the hall because it took lots of space. The mothers had double-dutched when they were girls, so they knew how to swing the ropes in wide arcs. When the ropes were the maximum distance apart, the friend hopped between them, spun around, then out the other side. Lila tried and tried but got tangled each time. She was disappointed, especially since the friend could do it so well. "It takes awhile to learn," mother told her.

Then the friend wanted to show off, so instead of hopping through the ropes, she tried somersaulting through them, but she got tangled this time. Lila felt better because this made them more even.

The doorbell at Lila's apartment rang the next evening. Father looked through the peephole then opened the door; the socialist woman stood there. "May I come in?"

"Yes, of course," father said.

She looked tired and depressed. "I have bad news, and I wanted to tell you personally...before you hear it from the media. Your son has been recaptured. He's back in jail, this time max security." Lila and her parents stared at her, mouths open in shock. Mother pinched her eyes shut and put her hand to her head. "I'm sorry to tell you. It must have been one of the government agents in the group...found out where he was hiding. And the agent must be quite high up...almost no one knew the hiding place."

"Can we see him?" Lila asked.

"No, they're not going to let any of us get near him. We can write him letters, but the guards will read everything."

"At least he's alive," father said in a monotone.

"We're going to do everything we can to pressure the government into giving him a light sentence. He's already a popular hero in the city. Now we're going to turn him into a national hero, a fighter for the poor against the corporations. The government doesn't want riots, so we can put some pressure on them."

"How much time could they give him...with the escape added on?" mother asked.

"Could be five years."

Father and mother shook their heads helplessly. Lila thought about five years...she couldn't even remember that far back. How could they steal that much time out of a person's life? "I still think there's some way to get him out," she said.

"Don't try anything," mother said. "It'll only make it worse."

"I'm glad so many of you could come today. It's a real show of solidarity on such short notice." The socialist was speaking to a group of about a hundred crowding the hall of an apartment building. "With all of us, there's a good chance we can block this eviction and keep this family in their home. And the next family...and the next. We're going to keep doing this, and eventually these apartments are going to belong to the people living in them and not to some rich investor. That's going to take awhile, though, and it's going to be a hard fight.

"We can expect the cops to be mean, but let's not provoke them. No violence on our part. We got a court order banning the use of tear gas indoors and banning pepper spray unless the officer is attacked. They can lie about that, but it's still some protection for us. That boy they tear gassed to death didn't die in vain. And those of us who got pepper sprayed didn't suffer in vain.

These things are painful, but you don't make a revolution without them. We all suffer and die anyway, so it might as well be for something worthwhile. If the cops are violent, get pictures of it, and we'll sue them. We're not helpless. If we're arrested, we've got a bail fund to pay your fine.

"They should be here soon. Let's take up our positions and be ready for them."

They broke into small groups and sat in circles, covering the floor of the apartment and the hall before the door. They linked arms with one another at the elbows, clenched their hands together in front of them, and interlocked their legs on the floor to build a tight mass of determined muscle.

Inside the apartment a group formed a human barrier in front of the door. They were each linked to their neighbors at the ankles by bike locks, and the two people on the ends were locked on to a radiator and a water pipe. They were connected above by a chain running through the sleeves of their shirts and padlocked at each end to the radiator and water pipe. The door could only be opened a few millimeters before bumping into the chain behind it.

The floor was also covered with people, and Lila, her parents, and the socialist sat in one of these groups. "Lila, I think you're the strongest one here," the socialist said.

"Good," Lila said, "I want to be strong."

The building manager, two police, and a six-man moving crew arrived in the hall. The manager stared in astonishment and said, "What is this?"

"It's a party," a man shouted to him. "The socialist party. You want to join the party? Sit down!"

The manager took out his cell phone to call his boss. Several men on the moving crew chuckled. They were getting paid by the hour — didn't matter to them.

One of the cops put his hands on his hips and said in a memorized monotone: "We have a court order to clear the premises. If you don't clear the hall or if you in any way obstruct us in our duty, you will be arrested and charged with failure to disperse, trespassing, disorderly conduct, illegal assembly, and failure to obey a lawful order. If you resist arrest, you will be charged with resisting arrest. Each of these charges carries a heavy fine and jail term. I'll give you one more chance to clear the area." He glanced around, more bored than angry — he was getting paid by the hour too. "OK, we'll start arresting." He spoke to the moving crew: "You guys help us. I'm going to get reinforcements and a bus to hold the prisoners."

They began tugging on people's arms. It usually took two of them to break one person's grip and a third to untangle the legs. Once pried loose, the person went totally limp, and two men had to drag them down the hall, into the elevator, and out to the street. The prisoner bus wasn't there yet, so they put the first few people into the back of their police car, but one cop had to wait there and guard them. Slow going.

Eventually more cops and the bus arrived, but it took an hour and a half to get to the apartment door. The manager unlocked it with his pass key, but as he tried to open it, it struck the chain inside.

"There's people here chained across the door," someone shouted from inside. "You can't open it."

The manager swore and banged the door against the chain, but it held firm. "I'll cut the damned door off the hinges." He stalked off to get tools.

"This is fun," Lila said, sitting inside on the floor. "Like a game."

"It's only fun if we win," father said.

"We'll win!"

The manager returned with saws, drills, and an extension cord. The cord, though, was too short to reach the electrical outlet in the hall. He swore and said, "I'll use the neighbor's."

He knocked on the neighbor's door, and when she opened it a crack, he told her he needed to plug his tools in.

"So you can throw that family out?" she

asked. "Not on my electricity you won't! Get out of here." She slammed the door.

The manager swore and stalked off to get another cord. Eventually he drilled holes in the door near the hinges and inserted the saw blade. Someone on the other side of the door grabbed the blade with pliers and yanked it out of the saw. The manager swore and put in another blade. This time he was careful to insert it only a little ways past the door, so it couldn't be grabbed. He started sawing, the blade moving rapidly in and out, but someone on the other side of the door held a file against the wood where it was being cut. Sparks flew, burning their skin, and the shriek of metal on metal assaulted their ears. Soon that section of the blade was worn away and wouldn't cut anymore. The manager had to insert more of the blade to get to a section that would cut. Then the man with the pliers could grab it again. He couldn't pull it out this time, though, because the manager had fastened it extra tight. But he could twist it so it didn't cut well.

Eventually the manager cut a half circle around each hinge and lifted the door out. Panting with exhaustion, he stared at the locked-on people blocking his way. "Good morning," a woman said with a smile.

The manager held up his saw. "I ought to cut your heads off."

"Don't blame us. Blame your boss," the

woman said.

The manager couldn't meet her eyes. Instead he picked up his bolt cutters and went to work on the chain and bike locks. This time the people didn't try to sabotage him. Too much of their flesh was too close to his rage.

Eventually the doorway was free, and the people inside gripped arms and legs. The manager, cops, and movers began prying them apart and dragging them out the door, down the hall, into the elevator, out to the street, and into the bus. As the apartment was about half clear, one of the cops got a call on his cell phone, then announced, "We gotta pack it in. Chief said it's taking too long. We need to do security at the soccer stadium." The other cops whistled in approval.

"What about this?" asked the manager. "What am I supposed to do?"

"You'll have to do it yourself," the cop said with a shrug. "You and the movers. We got orders. We can't spend all day on one little thing."

The cops left. The manager and movers stared nervously at the people. The people stood up. The manager and movers left.

The next eviction, though, the socialists lost. The cops and movers pried people apart for a half hour, then left seemingly in disgust. They just drove a block away, though. As soon as the occupiers left, the manager called them, and they came back and forced the family out onto the street. It was the family of the tall man who had got angry at the socialist woman. He stayed angry.

One apartment had a metal door that the manager's saw couldn't cut. To get around that, the police lifted two men up to the balcony in a cherry picker, a bucket-like container on a long hydraulic lift that could be raised high in the air. The occupiers inside saw them on the balcony and locked the glass door, but the cops smashed the glass, spraying the people inside with slivers. They waded through the occupiers on the floor and went to work with bolt cutters on the chains and bike locks blocking the door. While they were busy with that, someone went out onto the balcony and snipped the power cable to the cherry picker with wire cutters.

When the cops had cleared the locked-on people away, they found an additional lock had been welded onto the door from the inside, and their bolt cutters were useless against it. They talked to the manager through the door; he said he had a welding torch that should cut through the lock. One of the cops got into the cherry picker to go down and get the torch but found he couldn't move it. They had to bring another cherry picker to rescue the two cops and repair the cable. Then they just drove away.

In one apartment a man locked himself across the door with handcuffs he had taken from a cop during the battle to block the scab bus. But after they removed the wooden door from its hinges, they also quickly removed the police handcuffs with their standard skeleton key and arrested him for theft of government property.

One cop lost his temper and hit a woman in the face with his fist, breaking her jaw. Someone got a picture of the attack, but another cop saw that and smashed his camera. The cops all later swore that the woman had attacked him, so the case was dismissed despite the testimony of the people there.

Through the chat room on the socialist website, people could alert one another if an eviction was imminent and mobilize a flash mob to resist it. The owners counterattacked by hacking the website. While it was down, the people used mass SMSs to rally their troops. As in any war, each side learned from the other.

The government arrested as many resisters as it could and imposed the highest fines possible on them. As the socialist treasury shrank, so did supplies in the food bank. Workers who still had jobs made individual donations, but they weren't enough. People began to get hungry and discouraged.

The government learned of this through its agents and told the owners, who made the workers an offer: We will forgive your trying to take over our factories and the damage you did. Except for several communist agitators, we will cancel the bad list and let you return to work without a cut in pay.

The socialist woman pleaded with the group to reject this because it meant giving up everything they had fought for, and it showed the owners too were getting desperate. Without scabs the factories were running at less than half capacity, and that was hurting profits. If we hold out longer, we can win.

But some workers had had enough of struggle. They gave up and took their jobs back.

"If they had food, they would stay with us," the socialist woman told Lila.

"Then we have to get them food," Lila said.

"We don't have money for that," the socialist replied.

"The owners took our food when they threw us off our farm. Now they make us buy it back from them," Lila said. "We have to do to them what they did to us. Take their food. I heard they keep the food in a big building and send it from there to the stores."

"The warehouse, yes."

"There must be a lot of food there. We will take it."

"That would be very difficult," the socialist said. "They have guards."

"They had guards for my brother and guards for the scabs, but we took them."

The socialist was silent.

"We're hungry. We need food," Lila continued. "Either we take it or we quit. Then everything goes back the way it was: terrible." Her lower lip turned down in a grimace.

After a moment the socialist said, "Lila, I think you must have been Rosa Luxemburg in your last life." She laughed to relieve her despair. "You're right. It's either steal the food or lose the war."

Several nights later a woman with messed hair and smeared face limped up to the watchman's office on the loading dock in the rear of the food warehouse. "Help me," she said to the man behind the window.

Startled, he asked, "Are you hurt?"

She nodded. "Please help me."

He stood up from his chair behind the counter. "What happened?"

"I'm hungry." She pulled a stolen police pistol from her purse. "Raise your hands."

His eyes widened, his mouth dropped, his hands rose.

"Stand up and move outside."

He opened the office door and stepped hesitantly out.

"We are taking your food," she said. "If you

don't try to call the police, we won't hurt you. Otherwise...."

He nodded with a fearful scowl.

She waved to the others in hiding, and they drove up to the dock in a dozen vans and small trucks.

"Open the loading door," she told him.

He did, watching her closely; seeing she didn't seem violent, he relaxed a bit, his fear diminishing. "Hey, go ahead and take the food. I don't like the company any more than you do. It's a lousy job—low pay, long hours. Boss is a bastard." He gestured into the warehouse. "Help yourself."

"Thank you...for understanding." She stayed outside with him while the others looted the place, filling their vehicles with food. She and the guard began talking, awkwardly at first, seeking neutral topics: the soccer team's losing streak, the new movie in town. She put the pistol back in her purse but kept that clutched in her hand. They talked about the companies and the government and how hard it was to get by in the world. He said after they left he couldn't wait more than fifteen minutes before calling the police. She said that would be enough. They were silent awhile, then he said after this was all over maybe they could see each other in a more friendly way. She smiled in surprise but was too flustered to speak. She nodded. He smiled and said he could understand that she couldn't tell him her phone number, but when things were safe again, she could come by his window, and they could set a time to get together. She could even bring her pistol, if she thought she might need it. She said she didn't think she'd need it.

Putting the food in the food bank was too risky: it could be seized and used as evidence. So they stored it in people's apartments where others could come and take what they needed. People who never knew one another before became friends. They knew that to win, each had to help the other.

Now that there was more food, people stayed in the struggle. Some who had left now returned. Some workers who had kept their jobs from the beginning now quit in disgust at the overtime hours they were forced to work to keep production up.

The owners sent a message saying they would be willing to meet with a committee of workers to discuss their grievances. The socialist was elated. "This means they're really hurting. If we bargain hard, we can get changes."

First both sides wrangled about the composition of the negotiating team. They agreed that the owners' side should consist of one representative from each of the seven major factories in the city, but in order to exclude the socialist woman from the negotiations, the owners wanted the workers' side to be the same. Since she didn't work for any of the factories but instead for the party, she wouldn't be eligible.

None of the workers would agree to this, though, so the owners gave in. But in exchange they insisted that the head of the negotiations be the vice-mayor of the city, who was supposedly neutral but was basically on the owners' side. They would meet in a conference room in the city hall.

The workers who had been most active in the strike met to choose their representatives. They decided everyone who wanted to be a rep should give a short speech, then they would all vote.

"Who wants to go first?" the socialist woman asked.

Lila stood up. "Me."

The socialist smiled and said, "Lila, you've certainly done a lot. You've had excellent ideas and you've been an inspiration to us all. But these kind of negotiations are something for adults. Maybe your mother or father want to."

Lila gestured to her parents. "They can too if they want. But I want to."

"Let her talk," someone said.

"Yes, let's hear her," another chimed in.

"Fine," said the socialist. "I didn't mean you shouldn't talk, Lila. Go ahead and tell us."

Lila paced around, head down, hair falling over her face, thinking. Then she stopped and raised her head. "Adults have been here all along. If you could do it, you would've done it by now. If you haven't done it in all this time, why do you think you can do it now? You need some help. You need something new. That's me." She sat down.

The adults were silent a moment, wondering if they had been insulted, then a few people applauded. Others joined in. Soon everyone was applauding.

Lila was on the team.

The conference room in the city hall was high ceilinged with gold chandeliers and big windows. Lila looked through them to the park and court house where they had freed brother. It made her sad that he was in jail again, and it made her mad that the people in the government were the ones who put him there. On one wall were pictures of the men who had been mayors of the city, the new ones photos and the old ones paintings going back hundreds of years. On the other wall was an aerial photo-mural of the city showing all the skyscrapers but none of the poverty.

The worker reps sat on the photo-mural

side of the long, polished-wood table and the owner reps on the pictures-of-mayors side. The owners looked like the mayors, men in dark suits. A woman in a white uniform brought glasses of orange juice (*too sour*, Lila thought) and cookies (*not sweet enough*). On Lila's chair was a cushion that helped her not to feel so little. Her feet dangled in the air, but she was used to that. She was wearing the special blouse her mother had made and embroidered for her birthday, and her wavy dark hair was pulled away from her face with a red barrette.

The owners' reps smiled condescendingly at her, and everyone introduced themselves. Lila said, "I'm Lila. I work in the shoe factory."

The rep of the shoe factory, plump and balding, said with an indulgent grin, "I've heard very good reports about your academic performance at our school and also about your diligence during the business practicum."

"I lace shoes and put them in boxes."

"Yes, and you do it very well. I'm sure you're learning a lot." He leaned back in his chair and smiled.

"Are you the owner of the factory?" she asked.

"No, Lila. There are a lot of misconceptions about this idea of owners. There is no one owner. Our factory...and I think I can speak for the other factories too"—he glanced around at his colleagues, who nodded—"is owned by thousands of stockholders. They each own shares in it. A share is a little part of the company, and that's what they own, not the company itself. And it's democratic because everyone who owns a share can vote at the meetings."

"Do you own shares?"

"Yes, but I work there too. I'm a worker like you."

"How many shares do you own?"

He glanced away, then back at her and spoke with an index finger raised in gentle admonishment. "That's my private concern, Lila. We're not here to discuss private matters. We're here to discuss how we can make your life better. Let's talk about that."

He turned away from Lila and said to the socialist woman, "If you get the people back to work, we're prepared to give them a five percent raise. Plus if they're injured on the job, we'll pay half their wages until our doctor says they can go back to work. As you can see, this is a very generous offer, and we're not open to a lot of haggling about it."

With that, the haggling began. The socialist became the main negotiator for the workers, demanding a ten percent raise, time-and-a-half for overtime, full wages when injured, better ventilation and fire safety, and a retirement plan. The shoe factory manager did most of the arguing for the owners, explaining why such demands were economically impossible given the global competitive environment.

The lady in the white uniform brought tea and coffee and milk for Lila. "We used to have a cow," she told the lady. "I could milk it. But these men took it away from us. Now they give me a glass of milk back. And the cookies aren't very good." The lady walked quickly away.

After two hours the owners had agreed to six percent higher wages. They showed a PowerPoint about how higher labor costs would force them to close the factories here and move to another country. "There are lots of people in the world who would love to work for what you're getting paid," the leader stated sternly.

"Why are we talking about pay?" Lila asked. "I like what you said about shares. The company is divided up into shares, and people own those. How many shares are there?"

"Well, Lila," the leader replied, "it varies from company to company, but usually very many shares."

"OK, we take all the shares and divide them up among all the people who work there, same for everybody. Then the money the company makes gets divided up the same way. You don't have to pay us anything. We're all in it together."

"But, Lila, those shares already belong to someone else," the leader explained patiently.

"You can't just take them away."

"Who do they belong to?"

"They belong to people all over the world."

"If they're all over the world, how can they work in the factory?"

"They don't work in the factory. They buy the shares. The company needs money, so people give the company money and get the shares in return."

"So they own part of the company but they don't work," Lila said.

"Well, some of them also work in the company," the leader explained.

"You said you work and you own shares."

"Yes."

"Then that's how it's going to be for all of us. We all work and we all own shares. You wouldn't tell me how many you own, but from now on everybody has the same."

He drummed his fingers lightly on the table, patience waning. "I already told you many shares are owned by people all over the world. You can't just take them away. They're not going to give them to you."

"Doesn't matter. We don't need them. We cancel all those shares and make new ones. Only people who work own the company."

"How old are you, Lila?"

"I'm eight."

"Well, Lila, even an eight-year-old should

know you can't just cancel their shares. That would be stealing. You can't steal from people."

"Well, even an adult should know that it's not stealing. It's just taking back what they took from us. Our work makes the shoes and the clothes worth a lot of money, but we get only a little of that. Most of it goes to the owners. They stole it! They stole the money we made. Now we take their shares. We're the owners, so we divide it up equally."

The leader leaned towards her with a sneer. "We'll see about that, little lady." He turned to the socialist. "Now I see why you brought this child with you. It's a clever tactic, I must say. You're having her throw up an ideological smokescreen to distract us from the issues at hand. If you want a settlement, you better call her off and get down to the business of negotiating. We're all busy people, and we don't have time for these games."

"OK, brass tacks," the socialist said. "Six percent is not enough. There has to be overtime pay. We accept the medical insurance, and we'll wait on the pension plan until next year. But we want worker representation on the board of directors."

He sighed with relief. "Your demands are outrageous, but they're not insane like the girl's. We can talk about that." He turned to the lady in the white uniform: "Take Lila out and let her choose any movie in town she wants to see." He gave Lila a forced smile. "Any movie you want. And ice cream...whatever you want to eat."

"We'll do that later," Lila said. "We'll all have a party. I have some good ideas. But now we need to get the factories."

He stared up at the high ceiling with his mouth open. "I can't stand it."

The socialist said to Lila, "You can stay, but you need to be quiet for a while so we can get a good deal."

Lila nodded in sullen consent.

After an hour of hammer and tongs, the two sides reached a tentative agreement. Exhausted, they took a break and the lady in white brought drinks and doughnuts. Lila had kept her word and stayed quiet even though there were lots of things she wanted to say.

"I think this is as good as we can get," the socialist told her as people were wandering around the room in a daze of fatigue. "We got eight percent more pay, time-and-a-quarter for overtime, ventilation and fire safety, and one worker rep on each board of directors. Your father will be on the board at the shoe factory and your mother at the sewing factory. They'll get more money for being on the board, and they can bring up problems of the workers. They'll have a voice in the company. And you'll have a better life.

"The owners' rep and I will work together to

deal with labor problems for the whole city. The money I'll get from that will be a big help for the party. We've won!"

"Won what? Do we own the factories?" Lila asked.

The socialist paused. "No...but—"

"How many shares does everyone get?"

"Well, we don't get shares this year. We'll have to wait on that."

Lila shook her head.

The owners' rep—jacket off, tie loosened, sleeves rolled up—tapped his spoon against his cup and said, "Let's reconvene, vote, wrap this up, and go home." When everyone was seated again, he said to Lila with an attempt at a smile, "So the settlement has been explained to you. We all agree this is a fair deal. It gives people excellent benefits and lets them get back to work and get on with their lives. Now we're going to vote and make it final."

"We don't want eight percent," Lila said. "We want the shares."

"Speak for yourself, young lady," he said sternly. "All the other workers' representatives agree this gives them a fair share of the profits of the company."

"They should have asked me. I would have told them. The only fair share is an equal share for everybody. We need to take all the shares and divide them up equally."

"We've been through this before," he said, despair creeping into his voice.

"Yes, but you didn't get it."

"No, Lila, you didn't get it! What you're demanding is totally unreasonable."

"What's 'unreasonable' mean?"

"You can't think logically, you're irrational. That's not your fault. You're just too young. So you want things that are impossible. You don't listen to reason."

"I know the reasons. The reason we're poor is you own the company and you're stealing our money. The reason I won't do what you want is that would keep us poor. As long as you own it, we're going to be poor. That's how you get your money. And that's the reason we're taking the shares and dividing them up."

"I work there too!" he insisted.

"You work, we work, but you end up rich and we end up poor. No more. Now you get an equal share like everyone else."

The socialist, looking distressed, spoke to Lila. "We can't do everything at once. We have to go step by step. This is something we can bring up next year."

"If they don't give us the shares this year, why should they give them next year?"

"We can threaten to go on strike again," the socialist said.

One of the other worker reps spoke up.

"Realistically, people aren't going to want to do this again next year. I know I don't. It's too hard. What we're going to get, we should get now while we have the momentum."

Another worker rep said, "I'm beginning to think Lila's right in going for the whole thing now. That gradual, step-by-step approach sounds good, but it hasn't gotten us anywhere. I've been on the job twenty-five years. Every few years there's been a strike, and they give us a little bit here or there, but when things settle down, they take it away from somewhere else. Overall, things haven't gotten better. Like she says, why should they next year? Giving in now is just a way of avoiding a fight. Maybe we should dig in for the battle and stop putting it off."

The owners' rep broke in and said, "Look, if you want shares, we'll give each worker five shares a year. You'll own part of the company. You'll get dividends for those shares, and you can vote in the annual meeting—one vote per share. That gives each worker a voice in policy."

"I have a voice now: No!" Lila said. "It's our company. Equal shares."

Red faced and trembling, the owners' rep burst out, "Enough! This is madness. We're done negotiating. We vote now. If you reject it, you're cutting your throats. I promise you you'll never get a deal like this again. We will close these factories and relocate. You think things are bad now, just wait. There won't be any jobs in this city." He pointed his finger at the socialist. "And I'll make sure everyone knows it's your fault!

"Call the question. How many of the worker reps vote for the proposal?"

The socialist and two others raised their hand. The owners' rep glared and ground his teeth. "How many vote against it?" The other four raised their hand. "So be it," he said quietly. "You'll be sorry." He pointed to the socialist and said, "I'll never negotiate with you again. You put this little monster up to this. I know you did. You wanted to make a deal impossible, and you voted for it just to cover your tracks. Well, it's not going to work. We're going to crush this communist movement once and for all." Face twitching, one side of his mouth lifted away from his teeth, he packed his pocket calculator and stalked out.

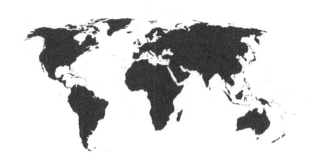

It took several days for the seven major factories in town to shut down. They finished the work in progress but started nothing new, and by the end of the week, they were all closed and the workers dismissed. The local and national media were full of reports blaming the "unreasonable demands and subversive tactics" of the socialist party for this disaster to the community. The mayor gave a speech saying if the party doesn't get rid of its radical leadership, it should be banned. The chief priest said the socialists' manipulation of Lila verged on child abuse.

The socialist woman called an emergency meeting of the party. "At this point it's either fight back or die. The whole power of the bourgeois state is aligning against us," she said. "To win now, we need to hold together in solidarity. They are already trying to split us apart.

"I'd like to apologize to everyone, but particularly to Lila, for something I did that split some of us. I gave in to the owners' lure of a better deal for me and a few others. I've been poor for so long, and the thought of a good salary swayed my thinking and made me want to accept their offer of a few reforms. But Lila set me straight. She reminded me of something I knew all along but had forgotten: We can't reform this system. As long as they own it, we're going to come out on the losing end. That's the only way they can make their profits. To have a decent life, we're going to have to take it away from them. We'd better start now.

"We need a mass march to city hall. Tell the government it has one last chance to act like a democracy and follow the will of the people. They must nationalize these factories before the owners can move the equipment out. The workers can run them. We'll make the things we need for a better life.

"The government banned our marches and rallies, but we have to do it anyway. Now is the time to get militant. Let's go talk to the mayor and tell her to keep those factories here. They belong to the people."

The party's call to action produced a wave of response. On the day of the march the streets were jammed with desperate, angry workers. They surged towards city hall like lava from a volcano that has finally erupted. People who had worked for decades in unsafe conditions for wages of bare subsistence were now seeing even that stripped away from them. Their lives were being crushed under the relentless juggernaut of corporate profits, their humanity sacrificed to the god of money.

The woman with two broken legs was at the head of the march in her wheelchair, accompanied by 150 people who had been disabled from work injuries. Behind them came the next generation whose futures were being mangled by managerial whim. Lila and her friend had organized the children from the factories and the shanties. They carried signs: "Stealing food is not a crime," "Poverty is the crime," "The owners are the criminals," "Free our parents," "Schools, not sweatshops," "We demand a future."

A block from city hall they ran into a wall of helmeted police brandishing clubs and TASERs. Water cannons waited at the ready. On the roofs stood more police, and helicopters circled overhead.

The injured and the children drew back. In their place came strong, angry adults, this time better prepared. Many had helmets and clubs themselves, and most wore towels soaked in vinegar around their faces to absorb tear gas. At the front the socialist woman addressed the police through her megaphone: "We are going to see our mayor. Since she won't come to talk to us, we are going to talk to her. And we're going to defend ourselves on the way."

As the demonstrators applauded, the chief cop thundered to them through his megaphone: "Disperse or you're all under arrest!"

As the demonstrators jeered, the police put on gas masks and began hurling tear gas grenades. The two water cannons blasted the crowd, knocking people over with torrents of high-pressure water. The wind blew most of the gas away, though, and the people knocked over by the water stood up and moved forward in soaked clothes and sloshy shoes.

Lila and her parents weren't in the hardcore group but on the edges of the crowd. She was perched on her father's shoulders so she could see.

"Charge!" the chief cop ordered his troops, who began clubbing and pepper spraying. The demonstrators fought back. Their helmets weren't as protective as the cops', and their skill with clubs wasn't as practiced, but there were more of them and more was at stake for them, so they fought harder. They dodged and thrust and parried, yelled when they hit and yelled when they were hit. The water cannons and tear gas stopped now that the demonstrators and police were mixed in the melee.

"Join us, don't fight us," the socialist woman called to the cops. "You're workers too. Your boss is the enemy, not us."

A SWAT team of six cops attacked her and the people guarding her, stunning them with electric shocks, then pepper spraying their faces.

A bolt of electricity knocked the socialist to the ground. Her body spasmed, then froze, almost paralyzed. She needed air but couldn't breathe. Her mind was a blank, she didn't know who she was. As she lay twitching on the asphalt, a cop hit her with pepper spray. She screamed and clutched her body into a ball, and they clubbed her on the legs and shoulders. They pried her arms loose, forced her hands behind her back, handcuffed her, and yanked her to her feet by wrenching her cuffed wrists into the air. "You're under arrest!" one crowed with a leer of triumph. "Assaulting a police officer." He shoved her towards a police bus.

"They're killing her!" Lila cried from atop her father's shoulders.

"I can't see," he said.

"Make them stop!"

Demonstrators formed a flying wedge, a V of workers that ran at the police in front of city hall, punching and kicking and clubbing the cops aside, finally breaking the line and running through towards the seat of government.

A shot rang out from the crowd—ka-pow!—followed by a volley of shots from the roofs. Two of the running demonstrators sprawled headlong onto the street, arms and legs thrashing. The people near them screamed and ran, falling over one another in panic. The other demonstrators stopped and stared up at the roofs. Lila followed their eyes and saw men with rifles. A spark of fire winked at her and became a crying wind past her ear. Another wink. She flew backwards onto the street. Father fell with her. Her legs were smeared with blood. Father jerked and twitched on the asphalt, face drenched with blood pumping from a hole in his head. He lay still.

Lila's mind stopped as if it had crashed into a wall. Mother knelt over father weeping. People were pointing at the roofs. Lila saw all this as if she were watching a movie on the moon. *My daddy...my daddy...my daddy....*

Rioters Killed As Police Shoot Back

Two rioters were killed and three wounded yesterday as a mob attempted to storm city hall. Elements within the crowd opened fire on police, who then defended themselves, stated the mayor's office.

"These are the same violent agitators who are responsible for the closure of the factories in the city," the statement continued. "They are determined to overthrow the rule of law, but a free society can and must defend itself against such attacks. It was only due to police restraint that casualties were not greater."

"Lila, you know you have to come out of this, don't you?"

Hearing the voice, Lila shifted her vision away from its glassy gaze and focused on mother. Her eyes drifted over the distraught, pleading face, held there a moment, then slid back to their catatonic stare.

Mother shook her gently by the shoulders. "Look at me." Lila's eyes met her mother's. "Do you want to come out of this?"

Lila nodded.

"Thank you, Lila," mother spoke through tears. "That makes me very happy. Would you like to go to the park, and I'll push you on the swing?"

Lila's eyes drifted back into space. She rolled onto her side, drew her knees into her chest, and gripped herself with her arms, shivering. She saw his smiling face in her mind. She would never see it again. He would never hold her hand again. He would never give her another hug. He wouldn't show her how to do anything. He was gone...forever.

Mother had father's body cremated. She held the urn with his ashes in her hands and thought of the years they'd had together: the wedding arranged by their parents when she was fifteen and he sixteen; getting to know each other and adjusting their lives together; gradually coming to love each other; the birth of four children, the death of two; working the land together, sometimes in despair when despite all their efforts the children didn't have enough to eat; the bad crop years, the loss of the land, the city; the struggle for survival here and its strain on their feelings for each other; finding a new closeness by working together for the revolution.

She set the urn in a place of honor in the living room, waiting on the burial until brother was free. Fathers should be buried by their sons.

The socialist party called a nationwide general strike to protest the murders and demand a judicial inquiry. All over the country hundreds of thousands of workers stayed off the job the first day, but when they were threatened with dismissal, most returned on the second day. The federal government banned the party as a subversive organization and froze all its bank accounts. This meant most of the workers who had been arrested would have to stay in jail because without funds the party couldn't pay bail and fines.

A rash of bank robberies and armored-car hijacks swept through the city and then across the country. Friends of those in jail appeared with cash to free them.

Lila's friend and her mother came to visit. The two women sat on the couch and talked and cried. The friend asked Lila, "Do you want to go outside and play?"

Lila shrank back. "Not outside—the men on the roofs."

"I brought jacks. We can play jacks inside." The friend took out a small red rubber ball and bounced it.

Lila's eyes followed the bouncing for a moment, then drifted off. *I don't want to stay in the bubble. But I don't know how to get out.*

When the socialist woman got out of jail, she came to visit Lila and her mother. Her head was bandaged and her shoulders and legs bruised. The three of them sat together sharing their grief. Mother and the socialist spoke a few words; Lila was silent.

"We've all had a terrible loss," the socialist said finally. "I knew everyone who was killed and injured, some of our key people. One of the police couldn't stand it anymore. He just went public and said the sharpshooters were told to kill specific people. And you were the target, Lila, not your father. They were trying to kill you, but they missed."

"Oh, don't tell her that!" mother burst out. "It'll scare her more."

Lila's face became alert and focused. She was with them again now and spoke in a slow, quiet, emotionless tone: "They did kill me. Now I'm dead. They can't kill me again, so it doesn't matter. They can't do anything to me now. They've already done it. Now I can do anything I want."

"What do you want to do?" the socialist asked.

Lila's lips moved as if to speak, then her eyes glassed over again and she withdrew into silence.

"I came back from the dead," Lila said, walking back and forth in front of a line of twelve police guarding the entrance to the shoe factory. "You killed me and my father, but I came back. He's still there." Behind her stood two hundred fired factory workers. To the side stood the socialist woman with a video camera. "Which of you murdered us? You are supposed to protect the people, but you beat and kill us. You are protecting only the owners. Whoever killed us, are you brave enough to say it, to tell me, 'Yes, it was me'?" She stopped a moment. "No one. Then you are not so brave. The man said you were trying to kill me, not my father. Well, now's your chance." She spread her arms. "So, no one is brave enough to shoot me in the open with people watching. You have to do it hiding on the roof. Not so brave.

"You are poor people like we are, but the owners give you a little more money, and for that you kill us when they tell you to. You are not so brave. You are just the trigger on the gun. The owners pull the trigger. They have bought you as their hired killers." Lila looked at the men: faces tense, mouths locked shut. "Instead of killing us, killing your own people, you should come back to us, join us, and together we can win over the owners. They are not really the owners. They just managed to grab up everything because they had money. We are the real owners because we make everything. It's our work. Help us to take it back from them. Don't kill us, help us."

She walked up to one of the guards, reached up and touched him in the middle of his chest. He stared at her, eyes wide, biting his lower lip. "Are you the man who killed my father? If you are, I forgive you...if you join us now."

"I did not kill your father, I did not!" He burst into tears.

"Then let us through. Let us take back what belongs to us. Otherwise the owners will ship it away."

He stepped out of the police line.

Lila took his hand. "You are a brave man. Thank you. Who else will be brave enough to stop being a trigger that someone else pulls?"

Another guard stepped out of the line. "I will join you."

The chief cop shouted to the others: "Arrest those men!" None of the others moved. The chief cop—face livid, teeth bared—strode forward to the two men. "Get back in line! That's a direct order!" The men stood there. "Then you're under arrest," the chief shouted. He turned to the other guards: "Handcuff these men. That's a direct order." The others stood there. Eyes bulging, he looked about him in disbelief. "You're all under arrest!"

All the guards walked away. The workers walked around the chief cop into their factory.

They checked to make sure the machines were still there, then posted their guards at the door in case the police returned with reinforcements. They took inventory of the supplies and materials they would need to start production again.

Lila, her mother, and the socialist left and took the bus to her mother's factory where the workers were gathering. Here Lila persuaded only three of the police to break ranks, but that was enough for the workers to rush past the club-wielding cops into their factory.

Mother stayed to help organize while Lila and the socialist went to the third factory, an electronics assembly plant. Here soldiers had already replaced the police as guards, fifty of them standing shoulder to shoulder with bayoneted rifles at the ready. Lila's speech fell on deaf ears. "They're from out of town," the socialist said. "They don't care."

The other factories also had soldiers now. "We liberated two out of seven. Not bad for a start," she told Lila. "The problem is going to be to hold onto them. Sending soldiers means the government is going to play hard. To defend what we've got, we need massive public support. The best way to get that is TV. We'll get our media people working on it."

The news that night carried a special report, a film clip of the police whistleblower describing how the sharpshooters were ordered to fire on targeted people as soon as a police agent in the crowd shot into the air. Then Lila was shown at her factory convincing the police to let the workers in. Then the city police commissioner was interviewed, saying that although the officer who made those damaging statements appeared to be mentally ill or on drugs, the department would make a full investigation of his charges. The police would continue to do their duty of protecting lives and property from violent rioters.

Next day socialists, anarchists, and other radicals from around the country began arriving in town, wearing helmets, rucksacks, and boots. The local socialists had welcomers at the train and bus stations to direct them to the two liberated zones. Lila reentered the shoe factory with them.

The factories became their homes. They slept on the floor on air mattresses, cushions, or folded blankets, washed up in the bathrooms, cooked on portable stoves, sang songs, talked about their struggle here and compared it to the uprisings that were beginning in other parts of the country: displaced farmers seizing state lands, thousands of renters refusing to pay their monthly tributes, armories seized and their weapons distributed to the people, pharmaceutical warehouses looted and their medicines distributed to free clinics, corporate offices looted, banks robbed, supermarkets robbed, hotels and restaurants for the rich robbed, police computer systems zapped with power surges, police cars burned, army trucks burned, air force bombers burned, homes of corporate executives and their politicians attacked by rock throwing mobs. So far these were just scattered incidents, but they were building in frequency and intensity.

Both factories were ringed by soldiers now, so no one else could enter. The doors were guarded inside by workers with guns, mostly police pistols taken from cops who had attacked them.

They tried to order new materials so they could resume production, but the suppliers refused to deliver. The electricity was cut off, so at night it was dark except for a few candles.

Telephone service, both land line and mobile, was cut off to the factories, but they could still communicate with portable computers via the chat room on the socialist website. Each learned that the other factory was in a similar situation: both isolated islands surrounded and under siege. Then the website was blocked along with several social media sites.

Through portable radios they learned that the socialist party had inspired workers in other cities to occupy factories owned by these two companies and had organized solidarity demos with thousands of participants. In response the government removed the party from the ballot of the upcoming election and jailed its national leaders for sedition.

Soldiers installed loudspeakers outside the factories and harangued the workers with demands for surrender. Their situation was hopeless, the loudspeakers blared, and the longer they held out, the worse their punishment would be. The chief priest of the town pleaded with them to give up. For the sake of their souls they should not offer violent resistance. They were being misled by an atheist ideology and should pray to the Lord for peaceful guidance. The Lord loved them but would punish wrongdoing.

Lila was lonely in the factory. She missed her mother and the socialist. She missed her father. The adults were nice to her and often asked what she thought they should do and often took her advice, but she didn't really know them. She was the only child there. At night she crawled into her blankets in a corner, curled up into a ball, and cried herself to sleep.

On the fourth night she was awakened by the sound of breaking glass. She peeked outside and saw soldiers on the ground below with stubby rifles shooting things through the windows. Something broke her window, spraying her with glass. It bounced off the ceiling and skidded across the floor, spewing gray fumes. She closed her eyes and covered her nose and mouth, expecting the burning sting of tear gas. Instead she got dizzy and everything started to whirl around as if she were in a pool of water being sucked down a drain.

She awoke with a terrible headache. She couldn't move her arms. She was lying in a pile of people. Her hands were fastened behind her back. Everything was moving. She was in a truck. Other people were awake too, struggling to move, moaning in pain. Someone was lying across her legs, but she wriggled out. "Knock-out gas," a man said groggily. "They hit us with knock-out gas."

The truck stopped; the rear door opened; gray dawn streamed in. Soldiers began dragging them out. They were in the soccer field, surrounded by a high fence. The soldiers stood each person up and took off their handcuffs while other soldiers pointed rifles at them. They were herded into a group and ordered to stay away from the fence. They could use three portable toilets and a barrel of drinking water.

Lila was still dizzy and her legs were so wobbly she could hardly walk. But when she saw her mother being unloaded from another truck, she yelled and waved and ran staggering to her. As soon as mother's hands were free, she picked Lila up for a hug, both of them crying in happiness, pain, and anger.

"If they put us in jail, we can see brother," Lila said.

"I don't think they will put us in jail. Look— we are over five hundred. That much space they don't have."

"What will they do with us?"

"I don't know. Maybe turn this into a jail. But then they couldn't play soccer. They wouldn't want that."

"I'm hungry," Lila said.

"So am I." Mother patted her empty tummy. "See my new blouse?" It was blue with red trim and puffy sleeves. "I made it there. I made one for you too. We all started making things."

"That's pretty! I want mine."

"It's still there...along with everything else people had. They carried us out with just what we had on. People lost all their things."

Lila shook her fist in determination. "I want my new blouse! We're going back and get everything. The factory is ours and all our things are ours and we're going to take them." Thoughts began to fill her mind. "I want to talk to the people." She started walking back and forth — this helped her to talk, to know what to say.

"Here, climb up on my shoulders," mother said and bent over.

Lila drew back, afraid to climb up. She closed her eyes and saw her father bleeding on the ground, the men on the roofs. *They killed my father, my grandfather — they may kill mother, me. But now it doesn't matter. I'm dead. I'm free. I will fight them.* She clambered up, unsteadily at first, and mother held on to her legs. "Everybody, listen," Lila shouted. "I don't have my megaphone, so I'll talk loud."

People stopped their conversations and listened. Many of them were still lying feebly on the ground. One person took a small video camera out of his coat pocket and began recording her. "They took our factories away from us again and took everything we brought there. They even took the new blouse my mother made for me there. They made our party illegal and said we couldn't be in the election. The problem is the government. It's supposed to be our government, but the owners have taken that away from us too. They own the government, so the government does what they want." She paused a moment, thinking of what to say. "It is not a good thing. So we need to take the government back too. The main government is in the capital, so we need to go there."

An army loudspeaker mounted on a truck began playing the national anthem loudly to drown her out. Then the music stopped, and the chief soldier spoke from inside the truck: "Some subversive adult has obviously filled this little girl's head full of dangerous lies. When we find out who did it, we will charge them with child abuse. It's a crime to twist the mind of a small child.

"Your government is democratically elected, and it exists to defend you, the people. Part of that is defending you against subversive influences from agents promoting violent foreign ideologies. It is our duty to get rid of them.

"Your government is not the evil monster that the subversives want you to believe. To prove that, we're going to show you mercy. Each of you here has committed crimes serious enough to warrant years in prison. You have committed these crimes either because you have been duped by the subversives, as this child has been, or you are a subversive yourself. But we're going to give you another chance. We're going to release you now.

"In case of future terrorist activities, though, we're going to photograph you and take a DNA sample. Then you are free to go. You must disperse and not loiter on the premises. This poor little girl is going to be the first to be released. Everyone line up at the gate."

"Everyone go to the capital!" Lila shouted before the national anthem drowned her out again.

Lila and her mother went home, ate breakfast, and cleaned up. "What do we take with us to the capital?" Lila asked.

Mother shook her head. "We can't go to the capital...too dangerous. They tried to kill you once already. If I lose you, I won't have anyone left."

"But that's the owners' fault. If we don't stop them, they'll keep on doing it," Lila said. "Is my new blouse the same color as yours?"

"Yes."

"I'm going to get it...go all the way to the capital and make them give it to me...and everything else. Then we can walk around our factory in matching blouses, and everyone will know we're mother and daughter and you made them. If they kill us, doesn't matter. We have to die anyway, and once we're dead, we're dead. We can't do anything about that. But now we can do something."

"But, Lila, we don't have enough money for tickets to the capital. We barely have enough money to eat."

"We'll take the bus for free. I have an idea."

With a weary shake of her head and a bit of a smile, mother took out two backpacks, large and small, and began selecting clothes.

The socialist woman phoned. She had just seen the video of Lila at the stadium and was going to get it on television. She congratulated them on surviving the gas attacks. Three people had died in them—never woke up.

Lila wanted to know if she was coming to the capital with them.

Yes, definitely. The time was right. She'd been busy the past several days mobilizing mass actions around the country to demand their party be reinstated on the ballot. Lila's speech was just what they needed to put people in motion. The government network would not broadcast it, but the commercial networks probably would. They knew it will bring viewers, and that meant money to them.

"When are we going?" Lila asked.

"How about tomorrow?"

"How about today?" Lila asked.

"I'll come by after lunch ready to go."

When she arrived with her rucksack, Lila said, "We're taking the bus."

"OK," the socialist replied. "But I'm not sure the party can pay for us all. We have so many fines now."

"We're taking it for free."

"How does that work?"

"I'll show you."

They went down to the bus stop and got on the next bus. "We're taking the bus," Lila told the driver.

"I can see that," he said with a smile.

"We're taking it to the capital."

"This bus just goes downtown."

"No, we're taking it to the capital," Lila insisted. "Everyone can come with us to the capital. And if they don't want to go, they can get off."

"Is this a joke?" the driver asked with a hopeful smile.

"No. It's a hijack," Lila said.

He turned to the adults with her. "Are you serious? Is this for real?"

The socialist looked confused for a moment, then said, "Very real." Her hand pointed in her coat pocket like a pistol.

"I know what this is about!" the driver exclaimed. "You're that little girl! That's why you want to go to the capital."

"Come with us," Lila said.

"I'd lose my job." He paused for a long moment, staring at them. "But ever since bus service was privatized, it's a crummy job. To hell with it." He rapped his fist on the dashboard. "This may be crazy...but I'm with you. We have to rebel...it's our only chance." He turned to the passengers. "How about it, folks? Anyone want to go to the capital?"

"We'll arrange food and a place to stay for you," the socialist put in.

Most people got off, but eight stayed, and the bus headed out of town. The socialist called the party headquarters on her cell phone and described Lila's trick for taking the bus. That way everyone could afford a trip to the capital.

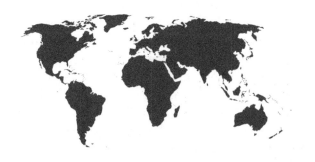

The call went out nationwide to gather in the capital and protest the banning of the party and its exclusion from the elections. People poured in from all over the country, sleeping in parks or with friends, determined to resist the government's assault on democracy. The police tried to arrest people for sleeping in the public areas, but they were driven out. Lila and her mother stayed with friends of the socialist woman.

The capital was much bigger than Lila's city and much more frantic. Everyone was rushing around and obviously no one was finding what they were looking for because they all seemed so unhappy. The air was full of exhaust. Each second a different kind of noise banged into Lila's ears. She was excited and glad to be here, though.

The government had forbidden all rallies, demos, and marches, but the party decided to defy them and go ahead with a massive rally on the great square in front of the Capitol building. At three a.m. on the scheduled day, hundreds of police used tear gas to clear away thousands of people who had been sleeping in the square. They tore down tents and raked them along with sleeping bags, air mattresses, packs, and camp stoves into a big pile and burned them "for sanitary and safety purposes." Then they surrounded the square to prevent a reoccupation. They in turn became surrounded by tens of thousands of people who began arriving for the rally.

Around the perimeter of the square the two sides faced each other in a stand-off between nervous police and angry people. Lila, her mother, and some of the socialist leaders stood on a flatbed truck protected by a squad of cadres who had been trained in counter-police tactics. A larger group of hardcores with helmets, clubs, and body shields, many wearing pistols and gas masks on their belt, stood facing the police line. Both women and men, the cadres had been hardened by years of police brutality. They had lost almost every battle, but with each loss they had grown stronger and more determined to overthrow this corporate government that was locking them into impoverished lives. Now with nothing left to lose, they sensed victory, and no one was going to stand in their way.

"We're going through!" one of them

megaphoned to the police. "We won't use our pistols unless you use yours. If you shoot, we will shoot. Move aside and let the people through."

They attacked immediately before other police could reinforce the line here. The hardcores charged, three or four to a cop, clubbing and kicking and knocking them aside, forcing their way through. The outnumbered police fell back or moved to the sides. One cop pepper-sprayed a demonstrator, who then attacked him with his fists, enraged but half blind. The cop pulled his pistol and shot the man three times in the chest. Another demonstrator pulled his pistol and shot the cop once in the head. People around them screamed in shock and fear but kept moving forward.

Through a breach in the line, a human wave of demonstrators flowed in to occupy the square. Some of the cadres stayed on the perimeter to guard the breach while the others ran directly across the square and attacked the police there, who were already battling another cadre squad. Caught between the two forces, the police line frayed, then parted, and another wave of demonstrators rushed in. Some cops continued to fight on the edges, going after demonstrators who had no helmets or clubs, battering them to the ground and arresting them. But they were often set upon by a group, stripped of their weapons, and forced out. Some tried to use their pistols to arrest people, but they were usually surrounded by demonstrators, many of them armed, and ordered to let the person go or be shot. "You can't kill us all," the people shouted. "If you try, you die." None of the cops wanted to die, which was fortunate because none of the demonstrators wanted to kill them. The cops released their captives and were allowed to leave.

Shielded by a phalanx of hardcores, the flatbed truck drove through the melee and into the square. From the back of the truck Lila could see the police, and she knew if she could see them, they could see her. She pulled on mother's hand. "Let's hide—over there." They went over to the sound system and hid behind the big speakers.

The truck stopped, and the party's presidential candidate, out on bail on charges of sedition, began speaking: "This square now belongs to the people!" A cheer went up from the crowd. "If there are any police still here, let them go. Don't hurt them but force them out. They have chosen to serve the owners, to guard the money and power the owners have stolen from the people. They are from the working class, but they are traitors to it. They don't deserve to be among us." He pointed to the thin line of police that now surrounded the square fifty meters away from the demonstrators. "First they tried to keep us out, now they try to keep us in. But it won't work.

We'll go anywhere we want. It's our capital and our country. Their days are over!"

The crowd cheered again. Several cops broke from their line and ran forward toward the crowd. They stopped halfway between the two sides and raised stubby, wide-barreled rifles. Tear gas grenades burst from the rifles and landed amidst the crowd. Shouts of pain and panic replaced the cheers. People tried to run, but they were packed too closely together. The grenades didn't have enough range to get near the truck, so the noxious fumes were diluted by the time they got to Lila, but they still burned from her eyes and nose all the way down into her lungs.

"Attention, police!" the candidate shouted. "We are going to defend ourselves. We have armed cadres on the perimeter. If you fire one more grenade, they will fire on you.

"Attention, perimeter cadres. Prepare your weapons."

Along the edges of the crowd fifty hardcores in gas masks pulled from their rucksacks small submachine guns stolen in raids on military armories. "Fire a burst in the air," the candidate commanded. A fusillade of automatic weapons fire rent the air. "Police! You fire one more grenade, and we shoot back. We're not taking it anymore. You've killed and gassed too many of us for too long. It's over!"

A shouted argument broke out among the

police, then gradually faded into silence. They stood in their line watching the people but not firing on them.

Demonstrators had called on their cell phones for ambulances to treat their wounded, but the police refused to let them through. Worker medics were busy treating the injured: bandaging a cut on a woman's forehead, rubbing ointment on burns from gas grenades; stanching the bleeding of a man's broken nose; giving pain pills; rinsing stinging eyes, noses, and mouths with glycerin water; clearing a woman's mouth of broken teeth. People were staggering around in shock or sitting on the ground crying. Two bodies lay side by side in a pool of mutual blood: one worker, one cop.

"We are suffering now," the presidential candidate spoke, "but we are winning, and in the long run that's more important. We are winning thanks to decades of efforts of thousands of people to build a mass socialist movement. But this movement has consolidated and turned militant right now thanks largely to the efforts of one girl. The whole country has been inspired by her speeches and her courage. The government broadcasters refuse even to mention her name, but her story has gotten out. Clips of her are posted all over the internet. Journalists all over the country want to interview her, but she's been too busy to talk to them. Her picture holding her megaphone is on T-shirts. Now here she is in person. Ladies and gentlemen, I give you Lila!"

She strode forward to cheers and applause, and the candidate handed her the microphone. Lila gazed over a sea of hair, heads, and helmets filling the square, then to a line of police separating them from the majestic white Capitol building with two marble lions crouching in front of it looking like they wanted to eat her up. She had never seen so many people. *Thousands and thousands. Enough to throw out the owners...if I can convince them.* Her throat squeezed shut; she couldn't speak. Then she gripped the microphone hard and forced the words out. "So many of us are here...and we are all banned. And not just us, other people are banned too. They banned my grandpa and father to heaven. Also a boy I knew from my factory. Also one of us here, lying dead now, banned to heaven. They banned my brother and my friend's father to jail. And they banned us from the elections. Then they banned us from being here, but we overthrew that ban, and we are here. Now we need to overthrow the election ban so people can vote for us.

"How can we do that? I could see this morning that they need us to work for them. They can't do it themselves. If we don't work, they don't make money. We can all stay home and tell them we won't go to work again until they unban the party. If enough of us stop working, everything stops working. Can we do that? Can we convince other people to stay home until we're allowed to vote for the party?"

A roar of affirmation came from the crowd. Some people started chanting, "General strike, general strike" and it spread throughout the square, each syllable reverberating like cannon fire and marching boots.

The candidate took the microphone from her and spoke: "Lila, you did it again. This is just what we need. We're going to take our government back and make it serve the people instead of the owners. Let's break into groups now and plan a general strike."

They divided based on where they worked and began organizing. But soon a dozen army tanks rumbled up to the square and aimed their cannons toward the crowd. Lila tugged on mother's hand and dropped down to the bed of the truck. Trembling, she lay flat and peeked out at the gray metal machines. Mother lay beside her and covered her with her arms. Lila squeezed her eyes shut. *Inside those things are men who would kill us. They shoot out a bomb and metal rips through us and kills us...like daddy but many more. Just to keep us from taking the factories. But we need to take the factories. Especially the one where they make the tanks. What we should do is change the tanks so they shoot just water. Then when there was some terrible fire, the men could drive close and shoot water on the fire.*

That's what we'll do with them. We have to change a lot of things.

Their truck started with a rumble. "Ladies and gentlemen," the candidate announced, "it's time to leave. But we are going to continue. We're going to bring the capital and the whole country to a standstill. General strike!"

Not all factory workers—seamstresses, shoemakers, steel fabricators—but enough of them, not all service workers—plumbers, auto mechanics, cooks—but enough of them, not all builders—carpenters, roofers, electricians—but enough of them, not all retail workers—cashiers, shelf stockers, counter help—but enough of them, not all transit workers—truck drivers, bus drivers, railroad engineers—but enough of them, not all government employees—letter carriers, clerks, teachers—but enough of them, not all technicians—computer programmers, electronic repairers, data analysts—but enough of them stayed off the job. They didn't stay home, though. They went to work but refused to work. Instead they talked to their colleagues about the necessity of the strike, the need to finally stand up to the system and change it fundamentally, not merely reform it in a few places, but take it apart and rebuild it. They argued that the short-term pain of fighting for this now was worth it for the long-term benefits for them and coming generations.

161

The value of their work could no longer be stolen from them by the owners. The government employees explained to their colleagues how the owners of the corporations were also the owners of the government. The teachers met their classes and taught them how they were being trained and indoctrinated to serve the system that oppresses them and shrivels their futures. Even some police and soldiers took part in the strike and pointed out to the others that their job was supposed to be protecting the people, but they were actually harming the people and protecting the power and property of the owners.

The employers and managers tried to silence them, but the strikers were very many and very persistent. The security guards managed to throw some of them out, and police managed to arrest some of them, but the end result was the work stopped or slowed to a trickle. The owners were losing money, mega-money. In some cases they lost their businesses because the workers decided they didn't want to strike—they wanted to work, but for themselves now. They seized the businesses and set them up as collectives.

The owners met with their politicians in a crisis conference, arguing about what to do. The hardliners favored the iron heel approach: the imposition of martial law and a violent crackdown by police and soldiers to restore order. Agitators would be shot, strike funds seized, food banks closed so the threat of starvation would force people back to work. The softliners argued that some of the police and soldiers had also been infected by socialist ideas and couldn't be depended on to repress the workers. If a crackdown like this failed, that would embolden the radicals to press for a full-scale revolution. It had been the hardliners idea to ban the socialist party from the election, but that had backfired. If they lifted the ban now, that would end the general strike. People would get back to work. The chances of the socialists winning the election were slight, since they were ranked third in the polls behind the two major capitalist parties, liberal and conservative. It would be less risky to lift the ban and then make sure they lose the election. That could be arranged.

The majority of the key owners—men of great intelligence, education, and experience in defending the interests of their class—deemed the softline approach to be more prudent in the present situation. The ban on the party was lifted. People went back to work. The election campaign continued, now with Lila giving speeches in support of socialist candidates. The party petitioned the United Nations to provide election observers, citing the government's violence against them and the strikers. The video clip of the policeman admitting that sharpshooters had been ordered to kill Lila and other party members and the clip of Lila confronting the police were translated into several languages and broadcast worldwide on news programs and YouTube. A global groundswell of sympathy for her and condemnation for the government convinced the UN to approve the election observers, over the vehement protest of the government, who viewed it as an infringement on their sovereignty.

The owners now faced a dilemma: If the UN observers detected their efforts to rig the election, they would become international pariahs, which would be bad for business. If they didn't rig it and the socialists won, they would lose the government as their enforcement agency. And more disastrous they would lose their property to the workers' councils the socialists were proposing. After much wrangling they decided not to rig the election but to do everything in their power to discredit the socialists. In the event they did win, the owners had been assured of international capitalist solidarity to overthrow the new government before it spread to other countries. Multinational corporations and banks would create economic chaos and blame it on socialist policies. Right-wing military units with CIA backing would stage a coup to restore order. If the coup failed, they would foment a civil war. They knew many tried and true ways to get rid of any government that endangered their property rights.

The campaign proceeded with the liberal and conservative parties drawing together in a united capitalist front against this foreign-inspired subversion of the national heritage of free enterprise. Religious leaders tried to persuade the followers that socialism was an atheist scheme and should be rejected. Rich celebrities endorsed the capitalist candidates. Two days before the election the socialist presidential candidate was again arrested after two undercover agents in the party declared in affidavits that he had raped them.

The people returned to their home cities to vote. Lila and her friend, along with their mothers, watched the election returns at the party headquarters with many other people. The mothers had made cookies and popcorn. Lila wondered if the corn had come from their farm. They girls were happy to get to stay up late. And late it was. Finally after midnight the socialist victory became clear—a narrow win but a clear one. The president-elect, out on bail again, promised he would represent all the people, not just those who had voted for him. The girls fell asleep while the adults celebrated.

Next morning mother and Lila went to the police station and demanded to have the things that had been taken from them during the knock-out gas attack on the factories. Two cops took them down to the property room and showed them a huge pile of "confiscated material." Lila went right to work burrowing through it in search of a blue blouse with red trim and puffy sleeves. She found it, wrinkled but unharmed, and put it on right there.

Lila had been afraid, expecting the police to be mean, but they were polite and helpful. Mother said that was because the people had won. The police would be friendly to whomever was in power.

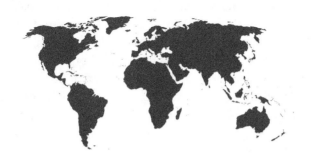

After the inauguration one of the first decrees of the new government was to free political prisoners and those who had been convicted of crimes against property but who hadn't attacked people. Lila, her friend, and their mothers went to the prison on release day. The captives filed out the main door in a long line carrying their few belongings in plastic bags, then through the gate in the high chain-link fence topped with spirals of barbed wire. The families and friends awaiting them cheered, but the ex-prisoners were mostly silent, blinking in the bright sunlight.

Lila saw brother, whistled through her chipped tooth, and waved to him. As soon as he was out the gate, she ran to him and hugged him around the waist. "Now you're really free!" she cried. He patted her head but dropped the plastic bag he was carrying. Mother hugged him and kissed him on the cheek. "You're skinny," she said. "They didn't feed you well."

Lila's friend saw her father—a tall, heavy-set man with curly black hair—and shouted with joy. He ran to her, grabbed her hands, and whirled her through the air, both of them laughing. He kissed and hugged his wife, and all three of them stood there smiling at one another. "At last!" he said.

The two men hugged each other too. "We made it," brother said. "They didn't crush us."

"They try, though, in many ways," the father said. "They want us to give up hope...and accept their power over us."

Brother looked anxiously around as if the guards might be coming for him. "Let's get out of here, go home."

The two families agreed to meet on the weekend to celebrate, then took separate buses home. Riding back, Lila watched brother, hoping he'd say something happy. He thanked them for their letters and for all they did to get him out. But after he said something his face would sink into gloom.

In the apartment mother showed him the wooden urn with father's ashes. Brother held it and chewed the side of his lip. "A good man. I can see that now...after some of the men in prison."

"I wanted to wait until you got out to give it a proper burial," mother told him.

"That could've been a long time."

"Nevertheless I wanted to wait."

"Dad...dad...." Brother's head sank over the ashes and he finally cried. A long time, shoulders shaking, tears streaking the urn.

The new government nationalized the major corporations and did away with class distinctions between labor and management. Everyone was now a worker with an equal voice in the company and equal pay per hour. If they wanted more free time, they could work fewer hours; if they wanted more money, they could work more hours. The government discovered, though, that the national and corporate treasuries had been looted. The politicians and the owners of the factories, banks, and corporations had transferred all the assets out of the country and then fled—a trillion dollar robbery.

The socialist woman explained to Lila that this was a disaster for the nation. They didn't have enough money to pay salaries or to buy raw materials for producing the things people needed. Without salaries people couldn't buy food.

"Where did the money go?" Lila asked.

"Most of it went to the USA," the socialist answered.

"Then we'll go get it. It's ours. We worked for it."

The socialist paused for a moment to consider this, then smiled. "The difference between you and the rest of us, Lila, is that you haven't been convinced that most things are impossible. Adults are filled with the idea they can't do what they really want to do, so they end up doing things they don't want. But you don't have those ideas. You still think it's possible to do whatever is needed for everyone to have a good life." She put her hand on Lila's shoulder. "And I hope you never lose that."

Lila stared at her. *How can grownups think it's impossible for everyone to have a good life? They must be blind. The things people need are there. We just have to get them to them.*

"I don't see how we can get the money back," the woman continued. "But I think going there and trying is a great idea. The USA is the largest capitalist power. That's where the really big owners are. They own the little owners who live here. That's how they got all that money out, through them."

"Can we go?"

"I think we can. The socialists in the USA have been working for many years to wake people up to what's happening. The owners have been pushing their wages down for a long time, and people are starting to fight back. Plus so many of them are dying or wounded in the owners' wars. They want a change, and they know the two big parties won't give it to them because the owners own those parties too. There's an election in the USA next month and the socialists are on the ballot.

"You were the spark we needed here, and you could be the spark America needs. If they go socialist, the whole world will. So let's go."

"Good," Lila said. "If the money's there, we'll get it and bring it home."

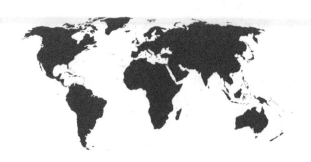

Lila had already become somewhat of a celebrity in the USA. She'd been profiled in the media as a child prodigy, and the videos of her speeches, dubbed in English, were widely seen on YouTube and many socialist websites. The USA refused to give her family and the socialist woman visas, so the new government issued them diplomatic passports, and the USA had to honor those to avoid an international incident. When they finally cleared customs in Washington DC after being thoroughly searched, reporters were waiting to question the eight-year-old revolutionary. One asked why she had come to America.

Lila had learned English in school, and as long as she could stick to simple words, she could do OK. She spoke slowly, pausing to think of the right word. "We came to get our money back. Our owners gave it to your owners...and they hid it here. We need to get it back." Now that she didn't have to hold a megaphone she gestured with both hands. "First we took back our work. The owners were stealing our money...so we took over the factories...but they gassed us and threw us out. They put a lot of us in jail. They put my brother and my friend's father in jail. They killed some of us. They killed my daddy...because they were trying to kill me.

"Then we took back our homes. When they tried to throw us out...for not paying rent, we all ganged up and threw them out.

"We took back our government. It was supposed to belong to us...but the owners had taken it over. When we tried to take it back, they killed some more of us. But we won. The big factories and banks belong to us now. But the owners grabbed all the money they had made from us...and sent it over here. We need it to run our country. So where is it?"

The reporter didn't know, but another one asked what else she planned to do in America.

"We're here to help you take your government back too. We won the election in our country...and we want to make sure you win yours...because then the big owners won't have any place to hide the money. It will belong to the people again."

"Would you call yourself a revolutionary?"

"Yes," Lila answered. "This is a revolution."

After the interview was broadcast thousands of people called the socialist party wanting to help. The government stepped up its surveillance and infiltration of the party.

Lila's family and the socialist woman stayed with comrades who had a big apartment in a poor section of Washington. They showed them the city, and it reminded Lila of her capital: great marble buildings and statues, green parks, big public squares, and lots of poor people living around the edges.

"How far are we from the ocean?" Lila asked.

"Not very far."

"Let's go! I want to run on the beach and jump in the water. I want to swim!" She held out her arms as if diving through a wave like her friend had shown her. "I want to play! But after we get our money back."

"I have great news," the socialist woman told Lila's family that evening. "You've got your farm again! And many other people have theirs too. The new government just passed a decree. It returns land to farmers who lost it to the banks. Now you have a home again."

Mother, brother, and Lila hugged each other in astounded joy. "It's ours!" mother said.

"I want to go home and feed the ducks," said Lila.

"But there's bad news too," the socialist continued. "The conservatives are trying to overthrow the revolution. The right-wingers in the military tried to stage a coup...killed hundreds of people and wounded the president...with help from the CIA. The fighting is still going on, could turn into a civil war. NATO has sent in soldiers. They say it's a peacekeeping mission, but they're really protecting the counter revolutionaries so they can keep on attacking us."

Brother stood up, fists clenched, forehead wrinkled. "We can't let them push us down again. We've fought too hard." He turned to mother. "I need to go back. I have to defend the revolution. And I don't want to be in this country if they're trying to overthrow ours. I have to go back and fight."

Mother closed her eyes, squeezing tears out the edges, then nodded her head. "If you must...."

The socialist woman looked dejected but shook brother's hand. "You'll be a good soldier. And we need you back there. I'll arrange your flight and contact the defense minister."

"I want to help too," Lila said.

"No!" mother burst out. "Don't go back there now. They already tried to kill you once."

"I want to help from here," Lila said. "This is where we need to fight them now. They took our money and are using it to overthrow our revolution. The people here need to know that so they can stop them. I'm going to tell them!"

And she did. In a series of TV spots made

by the party, she told the American people what conditions were like in her country and how the owners in the USA have gotten rich from that and are now trying to smash the revolution. She told them she had seen lots of people here who have jobs but are still poor, so the owners must be getting rich from them too. Those poor people need to take their money back from the owners so they can have a good life. The way to do that is to vote for the socialist party.

Lila said the things socialists have been saying for decades, but from her people could hear them and see how they fit their lives. They began wearing buttons and T-shirts with Lila's picture on them. They wrote songs about her. But some threatened to kill her, so the apartment where they were staying was guarded twenty-four hours a day. When she went out, bodyguards went with her. And she went out a lot — to be interviewed on talk shows and to speak at rallies for the candidates.

Each new poll showed increasing support for the socialists. Around the country workers began taking over their companies and declaring them public property. The Democrats and Republicans stopped attacking each other and united in a front to save free enterprise and the American way of life. The mass media which had at first fed the public's curiosity about Lila now turned hostile. Editorial commentators and TV comedians ridiculed her, implying that anyone who followed the political advice of a child must be dim-witted. The mainstream press portrayed her father and brother as violent thugs. The social media sites were suddenly full of reports that her mother and the socialist woman were lesbian lovers. Rumors circulated that Lila was actually a carefully constructed robot guided by the Illuminati. Preachers called her the eight-year-old anti-Christ.

On election night Lila was very tired. The popcorn was better this time but the cookies weren't as good. She fell asleep before the results came in: a narrow socialist victory for the presidency and both houses of congress. When mother told her the news in the morning, she said, "Good, when do they give us the money back?"

That turned out to be complicated.

The Bureau of Elections issued a report citing massive voting irregularities. It said the National Security Agency and Federal Bureau of Investigation had detected several cyber-attacks on the election computer system. Hackers had managed to falsify the vote tallies, thus distorting the results. But they had left electronic fingerprints, and the authorities traced those back to a foreign socialist government. The president appointed a blue-ribbon commission to investigate the charges of election fraud and foreign meddling. All the proceedings of the commission would be made public as soon as the investigation was completed. In the meantime the election was suspended and would be reheld after the investigation.

The socialist president-elect held a press conference condemning this as a betrayal of democracy. It was just a ploy to give the defeated government time to manufacture "evidence" that would justify overruling the will of the people and banning the socialists. Reporters questioned her about ties to foreign organizations and governments and how much influence they have in the party. When she said foreigners have no influence in the party, they asked, Then why are they here campaigning for you?

An article appeared in a British newspaper and spread immediately around the world, the transcript of a recording of an emergency meeting of the National Security Council. It had been recorded by a whistleblower, a White House aide who had sent it to one of the newspaper's reporters and then gone into hiding. The meeting began with a bitter attack by the vice president on the president for not having approved plans to manipulate the electronic vote count to prevent a socialist victory. The president had failed to take the socialist threat seriously, had ignored urgent advice to act, and had thus plunged the ruling elite into a crisis. The secretaries of state and defense joined in the attack, calling the president indecisive and inept.

The president accused them of 20-20 hindsight and said the vote manipulation plan was full of risks that they themselves had cautioned about at the time. Rather than arguing about the past, they needed to concentrate on solving the problem at hand. She insisted that the present plan—accusing the socialists of manipulating the vote—had the best chance of success. Many traditional Americans resented this foreign girl telling them how to run their country. They would believe that foreigners had hacked into the election computers and thrown the tally to the socialists. The government could portray this cyber-attack on American democracy as an act of war by the socialist country. This would give them the excuse they need to intervene with open military force in the country's civil war. The USA had fomented and financed it, but the right-wing rebels had little popular support and were now losing, despite the NATO "peacekeepers" efforts to protect them. A socialist cyber-attack would justify sending US combat troops to quash the revolution and would also provide legal grounds for nullifying the election. The media would focus public attention on the foreign interference and war, so the details of the election would fade from their awareness.

"If anyone has a better plan," the president

concluded, "let me hear it."

No one did. They broke into working groups to implement it.

The newspaper posted the recording of the meeting on the internet. It provoked global outrage, but the US government claimed the whole thing was a fraud. The aide was obviously a sleeper, an agent of foreign intelligence who emerged at the right time to destroy America. His socialist masters had produced this fake recording by having sound technicians manipulate voice clips from public speeches by members of the council. It was a socialist plot to divert attention now that their cyber-attack to rig the election had been uncovered. The aide's refusal to come out of hiding and take a lie detector test indicated he was lying. Other White House staffers who had worked with him stated he had expressed anti-American sentiments to them and disapproved of the ongoing war. "I never liked him, didn't trust him," one said. "He was a sneaky sort of guy."

The whole National Security Council appeared on television to swear to the American people that nothing like this had taken place. A blue-ribbon panel of twelve sound engineers from leading US record companies and universities declared the recording was counterfeit; two hundred sound engineers from around the world declared it genuine.

The public had had enough. From Alaska to

Florida, from Hawaii to Maine, they descended on Washington DC. When the hotels were full, they slept in Rock Creek Park, on golf courses, on the National Mall under the brooding gaze of Abraham Lincoln, in Arlington Cemetery on the graves of dead soldiers.

Two million strong, they thronged through the streets in all colors, genders, and ages, singing, shouting, and shaking their fists, a mass of humanity gathered to overthrow corporate rule and take charge of their lives. They rallied in front of the Capitol, defying the government ban on demonstrations. The police and soldiers concentrated on guarding key government buildings, but they kept a safe distance from the multitude, just circling above in helicopters and patrolling the edges in squad cars and on horseback. Sirens wailed from different directions like mourners at capitalism's funeral.

The president-elect spoke: "This great marble building before which we stand used to be a proud symbol of democracy, but it has become a place of shame, a symbol of the rule of the few over the many. We have to liberate this building from the big-business government that reigns here. We need to turn it into a true democratic institution, where the people rule both politically and economically. The people have to control the forces that bear down on their lives. Only when we have true political and economic democracy, where the people own the resources of the world and use them to meet human needs rather than generate private profits, will we be able to eliminate poverty and war. We've tried to achieve that with reforms, working for years for small changes here and there. But the changes were reversed whenever the owners needed to squeeze more profits out of us. We tried it through elections, campaigning and educating for years and finally winning, only to have victory snatched from us by fraud. Now we're just going to take it. We're going to take what really belongs to us — our government — and we're going to use it for the benefit of us all." She pointed to the Capitol. "We're going to go in there and clear the cheaters out and clean house. Anyone who stands in our way can expect to be walked on by four million feet!"

Instead of clapping, the crowd began stamping their feet. From the Lincoln Memorial, the Washington Monument, all the war memorials, the Reflecting Pool, the Constitution Gardens, four million feet shook the ground.

"Now I want you to listen to an extraordinary person who had a lot to do with our victory. Lila has inspired us all to do what we ourselves didn't think we could do: to win, to turn this country around. Now we need her to inspire us to take the next step and restore government of the people, by the people, and for the people. Talk to us, Lila!"

She walked forward as the crowd chanted her name, and the president-elect lowered the microphone to her level. She was wearing the blue and red blouse her mother had made for her, and her hair was braided with yellow ribbons.

This time the socialist woman had helped her with the English. For a moment Lila was too nervous to look at all the people, so she closed her eyes. *I didn't know there were so many people in the world. If I can get them going, we can take the government. I'll try.* She opened her eyes and waved at everyone, then spoke hesitantly, groping for words. "We're illegal here...they don't want us here. They broke the law...but they call us outlaws. Well OK...we'll be outlaws. We're going to take what we need...what really belongs to us. Some people say we can't do that...because they have more guns...and they'll shoot us. They shot my daddy...they shot other people...but they can't shoot us all. Getting shot isn't the worst thing. Everybody dies. If it's a little sooner, doesn't matter. The worst thing is being a slave to them. If we really want to be free...we can do it. The people who say we can't, don't really want it. They're too afraid...or they're really on the side of the owners. They should go home. And the rest of us are going up those steps into that building...and make it ours. Now!"

She turned around and pointed to the

Capitol steps, which were filled with soldiers, row after row of them ascending to the columned entrance of the halls of congress. Each soldier held an automatic rifle, and the distance between the steps gave them all a clear field of fire on the demonstrators. The plaza before the steps was full of police laden with clubs, TASERs, tear-gas and rubber-bullet guns, gas masks, body shields, helmets, and pistols. The people approached slowly, led by the president-elect, who was flanked by veterans from decades of war. Behind her were other socialist leaders, Lila, and mother.

"Fire the tear gas!" the chief cop bullhorned. Grenades lofted into the crowd, who now started moving faster towards the cops to get away from the gas. "Shields up, clubs ready!" the chief cop commanded as the first demonstrators approached. "Charge!"

The cops went to work: clubbing, TASing, pepper spraying. The people, particularly the vets, fought back. Some had brought clubs, stun guns, and pepper spray of their own; some were martial arts experts and used their fists and feet; some wounded vets used their crutches. One man had a propane torch that spouted flames, and he turned it on a cop who was clubbing a wounded vet on the ground. The cop screamed in panic as his clothes caught fire. He pulled out his pistol, but before he could shoot, two demonstrators clubbed him from behind and sent him sprawling next to the vet he'd been clubbing. One of the demonstrators emptied her canteen onto the cop's burning clothes; the other picked up his police pistol. Seeing this, another cop pulled his out and aimed it at them. They stared at each other and their gun barrels for a long moment. Then both shook their heads. "This is nuts," the cop said. He turned around and shouted to his chief, "I quit! Do your own dirty work."

The crowd cheered, and the two men who had been about to shoot each other put their pistols away and shook hands.

"I quit too!" another cop shouted. "I voted for these people."

"So did I," someone else called.

A cop threw down his shield and club. "No! To hell with your orders. These are vets. They risked their lives for us."

The demonstrators advanced on the rest of the police, many of whom stepped aside and let them through. "Stop them, stop them!" the chief cop bellowed in vain.

Some of the police joined the demonstrators, forming a guard around the president-elect and Lila, clubs and shields now raised to defend them. They all stopped, though, as they neared the steps and saw row upon row of soldiers aiming their rifles at them. The chief soldier stood in front of his troops, pistol in one hand, bullhorn in the other. "The game's over," he brayed. "Now it's for real—life or death. The police are one thing, but the 82nd Airborne Division is another. I'll give you one more chance to turn around and clear the area. If you move forward, we'll shoot to kill."

A helicopter with a big round disc underneath it flew above them and hovered over the crowd a hundred meters away. A boom of sound engulfed Lila, slapping and stunning her, drilling through her ears and eyes into her head, as if she were right in the middle of a thunderclap. Her mouth was hanging open but she couldn't get her breath. People were holding their ears and screaming, but she couldn't hear them although the sound had stopped. Then she heard her own scream, as if far away.

Then shots, a long burst of gunfire from the crowd. The helicopter tilted to the side, swerved in an arc, and slipped out of the air, crashing amid the people. It bounced once, rotor still whirling, tail breaking loose, then crunched down, spewing orange fire and black smoke. Pigeons were spinning through the sky and falling to earth. Demonstrators around her were collapsing in tremors, blood streaming from their ears and noses, vomiting on the ground. The breeze blew the odors of burning kerosene, hair, and flesh.

Those poor people...burning up!

The chief soldier pointed to the flaming

wreck. "That sonic cannon was a nonlethal weapon. But you responded with violence. So we will respond with violence!" He turned to his troops: "Weapons at the ready!"

The soldiers raised their rifles. Except for the cries of the wounded the crowd was silent. People began turning around and moving back, dispersing.

Seeing them drift away, Lila whistled through her chipped tooth and shouted, "Don't leave! We have to stick together. We can win if we really want to." Afraid, but knowing what she had to do, she stepped forward between the people guarding her and walked towards the soldiers. "We need to go up there," she told them.

"Fire!" the chief soldier screamed, gesticulating wildly with his arms. "Shoot now!"

One of his soldiers shot the chief soldier through the head.

Half the soldiers cheered and lowered their rifles. One of those who didn't shouted, "You foreign scum! Go back where you came from!" and shot Lila. Throwing her arms up, she fell backwards onto the steps, her blood pooling red on the white marble.

People screamed, "They shot her!" "They killed Lila!" Her mother, the socialist woman, and the president-elect rushed to her.

"Go now!" Lila told them, holding her side. "Now is the time!"

On the steps the soldiers began shouting and fighting among themselves. The new chief soldier picked up the bullhorn and barked, "Order, order! Fire on the demonstrators!"

Some soldiers raised their rifles and shot, and their victims crumpled down on the plaza. But most of the soldiers just stood there.

"Now! Go! Inside!" Lila yelled as loud as a wounded eight-year-old could.

Her mother picked her up while people around her shouted, "Do it for Lila! We're going in!"

The crowd surged up the steps. A few fell to bullets, but more soldiers were now with them than against them. They ran between the towering columns into the Capitol, and mother laid Lila down on the rotunda floor under the great dome next to the statue of George Washington. "Leave me here," she said. "Go on. Take the government."

Her mother and the socialist woman stayed with her, and a medic tried to stanch the blood that was flowing from her and staining her blouse black. The people thronged into the halls of congress but found no one. The magnificent chambers were empty. They heard sounds, though, like rats scurrying away. Their former masters were fleeing in their limos from the underground garage.

Several hundred revolutionaries stayed to

guard the Capitol, and the rest proceeded to the White House, arriving just in time to see the president and her family departing in a helicopter. The White House was surrounded by soldiers, but apparently after the fall of the Capitol they realized the people could not be crushed. Their strategy had changed from defending the buildings to defending the politicians in them until they could escape. As soon as the commander-in-chief was gone and the people were approaching, the soldiers marched off.

The tall steel fence around the White House, though, proved to be a formidable obstacle until a soldier who had joined their side fastened a hand grenade to the gate and blew it open.

Lila regained consciousness in the hospital but remained weak. The bullet had struck her side and shattered several ribs but missed the organs. Bone splinters, though, had pierced her liver and she was bleeding internally. Her mother, the socialist woman, and the new president visited her. "I have a big bandage here," she said, pointing. "It hurts. I can't lie on that side." She looked very small in the bed. Cords connected her body to electronic monitors, and tubes ran from her arms to IV bottles. Her face was pale.

They told her of the American revolution's success and that as soon as the CIA had stopped financing the civil war in her country, the fighting stopped. The government at home was building the new society in peace. The revolution was now spreading globally as socialists in other countries took power.

Lila smiled but spoke slowly, voice faint. "Did we get the money back?"

"No, not yet," the socialist woman said. "The big owners pulled another dirty trick. All around the world they took the money out of their countries and hid it in Switzerland and Singapore, where they are living now. The money belongs to us, but it's very hard to get it out of those countries. They have almost all the money in the world now, and we're broke. It's a big problem."

"No, not such a big problem," Lila said. "We make new money. It's the factories that make the money worth something. We own the factories, we own the money. Their money is nothing. We make the money and give it to the people. The world doesn't use that old money anymore. Maybe in those two countries they can use it, but they can't buy anything from the rest of the world with it. That money is dead." She gave a little laugh. "Not such a big problem."

The three adults stared at one another. "Lila, you're a wonder," the president said. "None of our economists could have thought of that, but you saw through the nonsense to the simple fact. We make the money. And we're going to distribute it equally. It's going to be something people use to exchange things, not to hoard up fortunes." The president took Lila's hand. "Thank you for solving this...and many other problems. When you grow up, you're going to be president...and a great one."

Lila slowly shook her head. "No, I'm not going to grow up. I'm not going to be here anymore. My light is going out. But we won, that's the main thing. And you can do everything now without me." The adults stared at her stricken. "My blood is running all over inside," she continued. "Things don't work anymore."

"Maybe the doctors can fix that," her mother said, groping at hope.

"No, I can tell. I have to leave. I'm going to get on my swing and go higher and higher and then just fly away. I won't have a body, so I can fly as high as I want and won't fall and break another tooth. I'll wave to you all down here. You don't need me anymore."

As the adults started crying, she said, "I'm sorry to make you feel sad. I feel sad too. I wanted to go back to our house and feed the ducks. The bank probably sold the chickens, but I bet the ducks are still there...and hungry. Can you feed them for me, mommy?"

Mother needed to wail her grief, but she forced it back to not scare her daughter. She nodded through tightly pressed lips and streaming tears.

"It's OK...not so bad, mommy. It's worth it. Now the things that happened to me won't happen to other little children." *I did it!* she thought joyfully. *I changed things!*

Lila died the next day, mother sitting beside her holding her hand.

The yard of their house was overgrown with weeds, and a "For Sale" sign from the bank stood in front of it. "We won't need that anymore," mother said and took the sign down. "Our home...at last it's ours again" — she paused, then continued with a wince — "or what's left of us." She looked around, breathing deeply, face thinner and sharper, more intense, than it had been five months ago. Tattered gray clouds were scudding across the blue sky, although the air here was still. "I forgot how wonderful it smells in the country. And the weather...sky so big. In the city I couldn't see enough of the sky to notice it. If only Lila were here."

The cow and chickens were gone, the corn had been cut, but the ducks came waddling out of the pond to greet the six people. Mother gave Lila's friend a bag of bread pieces and said, "You feed them. Lila would like that."

The friend scattered the bread over the

ground, and the ducks ran quacking after it, gobbling voraciously. Lila's brother, the friend's mother and father, and the socialist woman stood with them. The men held shovels in their hands.

Under the fig tree, whose blossoms of spring had become the fruits of autumn, they dug two holes near grandpa's grave. Brother set father's urn in one, and mother set Lila's in the other, which was beneath her swing. Beside the urn she laid the old candy box with her feather collection. "These may help her fly away."

Each person took turns shoveling earth over the urns. They all cried.

"Lila," the socialist woman said with a long sigh, "the smartest and bravest person I've ever known. She would want us to go on and finish her work. As she told us, The main thing is we won the revolution. We couldn't have done it without her. The world is different, much better now, thanks to this little girl."

"There's still lots of work to do," mother said with quiet determination. "The country needs food. I want to stay here where it's peaceful and I have my memories. I want to grow some of that food." She turned to the mother and father of Lila's friend. "What are you going to do?"

"Don't know," the father said. "Try to get a job somewhere...before the little one gets here." He patted his wife's prodigious middle.

"Have you ever worked on a farm?" mother

asked.

"No, but I could learn," the father said.

"Me too," the mother added.

"Would you like to live here, and we all work the farm together? The house is big enough."

They stared at her a moment, then smiled in gratitude. "That would be wonderful...yes," the mother said.

"Yes, thank you. This would be a great place for a family," the father added.

"It's so pretty here," the friend said, looking around. "And we can always think of Lila."

"You can have her room," mother said. "She would like that."

"But I can't live here," brother said. "I want to be in the city...work in the party. Father and Lila died for the revolution. I need to defend it. It's just beginning. We have a long ways to go."

Mother nodded reluctantly. "The city's the right place for you. But it's not so far away. We can visit."

"On the weekends would be good," brother said.

"And I hope good for you too," mother said to the socialist woman. "You might need to get away sometimes to some peace and quiet."

"Thanks," the woman said. "I need that...probably more than I know."

Mother managed something in the direction

of a smile. "Then we will all continue on...with Lila's revolution."

For more

For more "new energy" visionary fiction titles, including additional titles by this author, visit *Nascent Books* at http://www.nascentbooks.com

NASCENT BOOKS
CONSCIOUSNESS EMERGING

CPSIA information can be obtained
at www.ICGtesting.com
Printed in the USA
LVHW081120260220
648084LV00003B/4